TOM ANGLEBERGER

AMULET BOOKS
LONDON

THE SECRET OF THE
FORTUNE
WOOKIEE

AN ORIGAMI YODA BOOK

The Library of Congress has catalogued the hardcover edition of this book as follows:

Angleberger, Tom.
The Secret of the Fortune Wookiee: an Origami Yoda book / Tom Angleberger.
p. cm.
Summary: McQuarrie Middle School's students miss Origami Yoda when Dwight leaves for Tippett Academy, but he sends Sara a paper Fortune Wookiee that seems to give advice just as good as Yoda's—even if, in the hands of girls, it seems preoccupied with romance.
ISBN 978-1-4197-0392-8 (hardback)
[1. Finger puppets–Fiction. 2. Origami–Fiction. 3. Eccentrics and eccentricities–Fiction. 4. Interpersonal relations–Fiction. 5. Middle schools–Fiction. 6. Schools–Fiction.] I. Title.
PZ7A585Sec 2012
[Fic]–dc23
2012010027

ISBN for this edition: 978-1-4197-0517-5

Printed and bound in U.S.A.
10 9 8 7 6 5

Amulet Books are available at special discounts when purchased in quantity for premiums and promotions as well as fundraising or educational use. Special editions can also be created to specification. For details, contact specialsales@abramsbooks.com or the address below.

ABRAMS
THE ART OF BOOKS SINCE 1949

The Market Building
72-82 Rosebery Avenue
London, UK EC1R 4RW
www.abramsbooks.co.uk

DEDICATED TO JAY ASHER,
A WRITER SO BRILLIANT, HE HAS IDEAS
TO GIVE AWAY . . .

DWIGHT
(without DWIGHT!)

HOW CAN YOU HAVE A CASE FILE WITHOUT DWIGHT?

BY TOMMY

Every case file begins with a question . . .
The first time it was "Is Origami Yoda real?"
Then "Will Darth Paper destroy Origami Yoda?"

It looked like THIS case file was going to start—and end—with the question:

How can you have a case file without Dwight?

Because Dwight's the guy who made Origami Yoda in the first place. And it was Origami Yoda who made so much interesting stuff happen that was worth investigating.

The first case file I ever made was when Origami Yoda first showed up. I got other kids

DWIGHT

ORIGAMI YODA   THE FORCE   FLOATING ROCK

at McQuarrie Middle School to tell their stories about him and it proved (sort of) that Origami Yoda was real and could really use the Force.

With the second case file, we (sort of) saved Dwight from getting sent to reform school. But he did end up getting suspended until January, so he did end up at a different school, and he took Origami Yoda with him.

Things seem like they have worked out pretty well for Dwight. He's at Tippett Academy, where that girl he likes JUST HAPPENS to go. Well, that's nice for Dwight . . . but what about the rest of us? We're still stuck here at McQuarrie Middle School without Origami Yoda

DUMB STUFF DO NOT!

to keep us from doing dumb stuff and telling us the not-dumb stuff we should be doing.

The first day back to school without Dwight, Kellen and I were wondering if anything interesting enough to write (and doodle) about was ever going to happen again.

It definitely seemed like all the fun was

SO.... BORED...

over. Plus my semi-girlfriend, Sara, and Kellen's dream-semi-girlfriend, Rhondella, kept whispering with the other girls and hardly spoke to us. And without Origami Yoda's help,

we had no idea what to say to them. (Although I think Kellen successfully proved that a ten-minute lecture about why Boba didn't die in the Sarlacc pit is what NOT to say to them.)

Harvey had plenty to say, of course. He always does. And it's always boring. And loud. And usually rude. And now that Origami Yoda was gone, his Darth Paper didn't have much to do, which was a relief, but also kind of boring . . . z z²²

"If you can't write a case file, that means I can't draw on your case file," said Kellen. "What are we going to do?"

"Maybe you could finally finish drawing the pictures for that graphic novel I wrote," I said.

"Uh, you mean the cowboys who ride around on snails? No offense, man, but that thing

LINOLEUM FLOORING →

is boring like linoleum flooring! We've got to find SOMETHING to write a case file about!"

Well, we didn't find anything that day. But the next day we found something . . . a BIG something . . . a BIG HAIRY something: the Fortune Wookiee.

And that meant we had a question to answer: Can an origami Chewbacca possibly be as helpful as Origami Yoda?

So we got to work on a case file about it right away.

At first it looked like this would be a case file without Dwight, which seemed kind of sad. But before long we started having Dwight Sightings, so it looked like everything was back to normal.

But of course where Dwight is involved, nothing is ever normal.

BINOCULARS

Harvey's Comment

So far it looks like the real question is going to be: can this case file be even lamer than the last two?

4

RISE OF THE FORTUNE WOOKIEE

BY TOMMY

Day Two of the Post-Dwight Era started the same way: me and Kellen sitting around in the library wondering if boredom had engulfed the school forever. (Harvey was busy—annoying us.)

It was just the beginning of November, and Dwight would be gone at least until January, and probably forever! I mean, why would he come back? He was at Tippett Academy, which not only had his girlfriend but was also supposed to be a really expensive private

school with fancy lunches and cool classes and stuff.

Meanwhile, we were stuck here at a school ruled by Principal Rabbski, who is basically like the Emperor, only meaner and without the lightning bolts.

AND most of the other kids here either think we're weirdos or wimps or simply aren't aware of our existence until we do something that annoys them.

AND our lunches are gross.

AND we don't have Origami Yoda to help us.

AND on top of all that, as I may have said earlier, things are totally boring!

AND then . . .

"Hey, guys!" called Sara, as she headed for our table. "Check this out!"

She held up this weird thing. It was sort of like an origami finger puppet. But it sure wasn't Yoda—it was brown.

All of a sudden, it opened its mouth.

"MMMMMRRRRRWTTTTTHHHH!"

"Holy furballs!" said Kellen. "It's Chewbacca!"

"Yeah!" said Sara. "Dwight made it for us.
He yelled at me from his bedroom window while
I was waiting for the bus this morning. Then
he threw it down to me in a plastic baggie."

"Do it again!" said Kellen.

"Mmmrrrgggggg!" went Sara, opening Chewie's
mouth. There were fangs in there!

"Uh," said Harvey. Whenever he starts a
sentence with "Uh," you know he's about to be
obnoxious. "First of all, that's not all one
piece of uncut paper, so it's kirigami, NOT
origami! And why does he have a crack down
the middle of his face?"

Harvey was right: Chewie's head seemed
to be in separate sections. Since Dwight
is a super-awesome origami folder, I was
surprised that he hadn't figured out a way
to make Chewbacca without a crack down his
face.

"That's the best part," said Sara. "This

isn't just a puppet, it's a fortune teller. Dwight called it a Fortune Wookiee."

Harvey rolled his eyes. "Great, guess what your fortune is? Mmmrrrrwwwwggh! That's almost as helpful as Paperwad Yoda's stupid predictions."

"Uh," Kellen said, in perfect imitation of Harvey. "You may remember that Paperwad Yoda's predictions always came true."

"Always? How about—" started Harvey.

"All right, boys," growled Sara's best friend, Rhondella. "Do you want to hear what Chewie has to say or not?"

"Yes!" said me and Kellen—and Lance, Amy, and Quavondo, who had come over to see what was going on.

"Well, it works just like a regular fortune teller," said Sara.

"Like a what?"

"A fortune teller. You know," she said.

We didn't know.

"Do you mean you guys don't know what

TRUE THEY CAME, YES!

FORTUNE TELLER

8

COOTIE CATCHER

that is?" said Rhondella. "It's a cootie catcher. You guys run around 'origami this' and 'origami that' and you don't know about cootie catchers?"

"No, but you can tell us," said Kellen. See, he's in love with Rhondella, and she usually doesn't even speak to him because she's still mad about something, so he was trying to suck up.

SAD BUT TRUE!

Do you see how complicated things are at this school? Do you see why we need help?

Anyway, Sara showed us how it worked.

"Which *Star Wars* movie is your favorite? Episode what?"

"Five! *The Empire Strikes Back*," I said.

She held the Fortune Wookiee with both hands and made it open its mouth. "One." Then she closed it and opened it the other way, right down the center of his face. "Two." Then the mouth again. "Three." The face again. "Four." And the mouth again. "Five."

When she finished, she kept it open.

ONE

TWO

YUCK!

TRIANGLES

"Now look into his mouth. You see the four triangles inside?"

"Yes."

"Okay. Name a *Star Wars* character."

I thought for a second, then said, "Wicket."

"Wicket?" sneered Harvey. "You picked Wicket? Out of the whole *Star Wars* Expanded Universe, you picked an Ewok?"

"It just popped into my head."

"Good," said Sara. "That's how it's supposed to work. Now watch."

She put her finger on a triangle and said "W."

Then the next triangle. "I." And she went around clockwise, moving her finger one triangle for each letter: "C-K-E-T."

"Now, if we were really doing this," she said, "we'd lift up the triangle I stopped on and see what Dwight wrote underneath."

"Let's see," I said. "What's it say?"

"No," said Sara. "Dwight told me to only use it for emergencies."

"Emergencies?" said Harvey. "Hey, I just broke my leg. Will you ask your cootie catcher to save me?"

"You know what I mean," said Sara. "And I'm sure Dwight didn't expect YOU to ask the Fortune Wookiee a question, Harvey. I'm sure he expected you to make fun of it."

"Hey! He finally got a prediction right!" whooped Harvey, way too loud. Mrs. Calhoun, the librarian, started walking over to tell us to be quiet. I wonder if she ever gets tired of having to do that?

Harvey's Comment

Actually, the so-called cootie catcher is really a traditional Japanese fold called a salt cellar. ←

Tommy's Comment: Thanks for that thrilling piece of information, Harvey! As usual, your comments add SO much!

SALT

R.I.P.
ORIGAMI

REVENGE OF
THE RABBSKI

BY HARVEY

Scene: Library

When: Two seconds after the last chapter ended

Before Mrs. Calhoun got to us, we heard another voice coming up behind us . . . a voice that strikes fear in the hearts of all decent people . . . a voice that is like a disturbance in the Force!

"Sara, I didn't expect you to be the one holding a *Star Wars* puppet."

It was Principal Rabbski!

Where had she come from? I seriously think she has some kind of Sith powers. (Well, no, not seriously.)

"Well, I'm sure you kids have heard all sorts of stories about why Dwight isn't here." She glared at me and Tommy. "That origami Yoda of his wasn't the reason he was suspended, but it WAS a major disruption of the learning environment.

"You all know our school policies. You're here to learn, and it's my job to eliminate disruptions and distractions. That's why we're going to have a new policy. All this origami stuff is neat, but it belongs at home. Keep it at home, or I will take it away. No puppets, no paper airplanes, no folded paper of any kind. Let's try to get off to a fresh start, okay?"

Well, that's the most outrageous thing ever! You can't stop people from folding a piece of paper! What is she going to do, arrest Lunchman Jeff for giving out napkins in the cafeteria? Napkins are folded paper, so they are origami! Anytime you fold paper, that's origami. Books? Folded paper! Report cards? Folded paper! Envelopes? Folded paper!

Toilet paper? Not origami because it is rolled, not folded! But a million other things are origami!

"Ms. Rabbski, this is totally unfair," I said. "I'm practically an origami master."

13

"You, Harvey, are the last person who should be speaking right now. You and your Darth Vader have caused almost as much trouble around here as the origami Yoda did."

"He's not Darth PAPER anymore," I said, holding him up. "He's Anakin again. See how the helmet lifts up to show—"

"This is exactly what I'm talking about!" said Rabbski, and she yanked Darth Paper/Anakin right off my finger! "Distractions. You're so distracted by this stuff, you aren't even listening. I don't care WHO your puppet is, it doesn't belong in school. No more origami at school. It's that simple."

I was already thinking about how I was going to sue the school. But then the strangest thing happened . . .

"I don't think I can agree with that, Ms. Rabbski."

It was the librarian, Mrs. Calhoun!

"Excuse me?" said Rabbski.

"I'm not big on banning things in the library," Calhoun said. "Anytime the kids are learning something in here, that's a good thing. And we have

MRS. CALHOUN

a nice section of origami books in here now, because the kids have been so interested in it lately."

For a second, I thought Rabbski was going to do a Vader force choke grip on Mrs. Calhoun. And then a couple more seconds went by with nothing happening. Finally, Rabbski made this little bow at Mrs. Calhoun. Just a slow head nod sort of thing.

"Okey-dokey," she said. "If you don't mind them doing it in here, that's fine. But that's it. If I hear about more problems in the classrooms or see you guys waving them around at lunch or in the hall, they're mine."

She gave me back Darth Paper and then left. And Mrs. Calhoun—who I thought was only interested in making sure we didn't use the computers for games —became our hero.

"Name any *Star Wars* character you want, Mrs. Calhoun!" I said. "I'll make it for you."

"Well, thank you, Harvey! How about General Grievous?" she asked.

Man, he's going to be hard to make with those four arms. I'm still working on it.

My Comment: It's weird that I never thought about it before, but we do have a lot of origami books, and *Star Wars* books, too. And Mrs. Calhoun must be the one who buys them. I had no idea she was paying attention. I thought her only interest was in telling me and Kellen to "keep it down to a dull roar."

HAN FOLDO

BY TOMMY

After Rabbski left, Sara showed us an origami Han Solo finger puppet. She called it Han Foldo.

"Han Foldo?" sneered Harvey. "What kind of a name is Han Foldo? That's the dumbest thing I ever heard."

Sara glared at him and started to put Han Foldo away.

"Wait!" me and Kellen said. "We want to see it."

"Too bad," she said, and started to pile up her books and leave.

I'M NICE NOW!

"All right, all right," said Harvey. "I'm sorry. It's not the dumbest thing I ever heard." (That's Harvey's idea of being a nice guy, now that he has escaped the Dark Side. He still has a loooooooooong way to go.)

"What does Han do, anyway?" asked Lance.

So Sara got him back out and said that he was going to interpret Chewbacca's roars and growls for us.

Harvey snorted and Han Foldo said, "Laugh it up, Fuzzball!"

Sara said she was only going to use Chewie and Han Foldo in the library, so she didn't get in trouble with Rabbski. Anybody could come see her in the library before school anytime we had a real, actual, important question.

Harvey's Comment

→ okay, I'm sorry, but Han Foldo is lame.

It was one thing when Dwight drew a face on his emergency Yoda. And, yes, I drew some lines on my

18

Darth Paper. But Han Foldo is basically just a square that has hair, a face, and a vest glued on it. That's not real origami.

And the name? Han Foldo? Really?

My Comment: Uhhh . . . Han Foldo's not origami????
I seem to remember a certain smarty-pants saying that "origami is folded paper! Anytime you fold paper, that's origami."

Besides, Han SOLO is the opposite of lame. So Han FOLDO can't be lame.

At this point, I was just writing these case file sections out of habit, and letting Harvey and Kellen make their contributions. I didn't know they were going to develop into a real investigation. It seemed like we might as well gather other kids' Fortune Wookiee experiences, if there were any. Sure enough, the next day, Lance had a real, actual, important question. In fact, it was basically a real, actual, important EMERGENCY . . .

FORTUNE WOOKIEE BOOGIE-WOOGIE

BY LANCE

I had a problem and I really, really, really wanted Origami Yoda's help.

But no Dwight meant no Yoda, so I was willing to give Fortune Wookiee a try. I was desperate. But to go up to Sara and explain it all to her so that she could give me the Fortune Wookiee's advice . . . that was embarrassing. I wouldn't have minded explaining my secret to Dwight. I knew he wouldn't laugh at me.

But it was the Fortune Wookiee or nothing, so I had to talk to Sara. And I had to do it first thing in the morning, because I knew all heck was about to break loose at school that day. Things would get a million times more embarrassing if I didn't do something right away.

I found her in the library with Tommy and asked her to come to a different table so I could ask her something. Tommy glared at me, but I was like, "Sorry, dude, this is serious stuff."

Sara and I moved to the next table.

"Will you promise not to tell Amy?" I whispered.

"Okay, sure," she said.

"What about Tommy? You won't tell him, will you? Even though he's your—"

AMY

"No," she said, "I won't tell Tommy. Good grief, what's the big deal?"

"Well," I said, and looked around to make sure no one was listening. It's hard to get a minute of privacy in this school! "Well, you know how I've been taking karate lessons for a couple of years?"

"Uh, I guess."

"Well, they aren't exactly karate lessons."

"What are they?" she asked. "Ballet lessons?"

I was like, "AAAAH! SHHHHH! How did you know?"

"I didn't know. I just said the silliest thing I could think of. Are you REALLY taking ballet lessons?"

"Yes," I said. "And tap."

"Tap? You tap-dance?"

"Yeah," I said.

So I told Sara about how it all got started. A couple of years ago, I really did take karate lessons. Or actually, one karate lesson. Over at Debbie-Don's Dance Dojo. Miss Debbie teaches dance, and her husband, Don, teaches Korean karate.

My mother got these coupons off the Internet for free introductory classes. She had the idea for me to try Korean karate while my little sister took tap. Well, Grace decided she wanted to take Korean karate, too.

So we were both in the same free introductory class, and Don kept going on and on about how great Grace was. He just told me not to fidget so much.

Then it was time for Grace's free introductory tap class. Mom and I sat on folding chairs to watch. I couldn't believe it when Miss Debbie started dancing. She was awesome.

So . . . Grace takes Korean karate. I take tap. And Miss Debbie said I was so good, I should take ballet, too, especially since she really needs boys in ballet.

I thought I was safe since Debbie-Don's is all the way over on Williamson Road. Nobody else from our school was going there.

Until now.

"Last night, Jen was at Debbie-Don's! She's taking lessons from Miss Debbie, too!" I said. "She's going to tell everybody!"

"I don't mean to be rude, but does Jen even know who you are?" asked Sara.

"Yes. There was an incident in the cafeteria in fifth grade. It involved a pudding cup. She hasn't forgiven me. This is her chance to humiliate me! She may be telling Harvey right now!"

"Wow, what are you going to do?"

"I don't know! That's why I'm asking you to use the Fortune Wookiee. I've got to stop her."

"Okay, let's see what he says."

She asked my favorite *Star Wars* movie: *Episode III: Revenge of the Sith*! Then favorite character: Boba Fett.

Eight letters. Sara spelled them out while she pointed to the triangles. When she got to the end of Fett, she lifted up the triangle she was pointing to and read what was underneath.

"Rooooarr!"

"What does that mean?" I asked.

Han Foldo said, "Wookiees ain't modest, kid."

"I didn't say they were."

"Well, they ain't!"

"Okay! Okay! What does that mean?"

"I guess it means they boast and brag a lot," said Sara.

"I meant . . . what good does that do me?"

"I think I get it," Sara said. "Instead of being embarrassed, you're supposed to be proud of it. Brag about it!"

"Hey, Lance!" It was Harvey! With a jumbo smirk! Jen must have already told him.

Tommy and Kellen looked up from the Pencil Podrace game they were playing. Mike and Quavondo were watching from the computer table. And Amy just appeared from nowhere! Great, everybody was going to laugh at me! People were going to forget all about Dwight, and I was going to go down in history as the weirdest kid in the history of the school!

"Guys, you won't BE-LIEVE this," said Harvey. "Lance takes dance lessons!"

I was about to deny it, but then Sara whispered, "This is it! Either be a wimp or a Wookiee."

I decided to be a Wookiee.

WIMP -or- WOOKIEE!

I turned around and looked at Harvey. Right at him. Any sign of shame would give him a chance to spring for the kill. He was ready to unload a bunch of tutu jokes, I could tell.

"What YOU won't be-lieve, Harvey," I said, loud enough for all of them to hear, "is how good I am."

"WHAT?"

The smirk disappeared. I knew I had won.

"You're good at it?" asked Tommy.

"I'm great!"

"Prove it," said Harvey.

click

So I did. It didn't sound as good without my tap shoes, but it was pretty loud on the linoleum. I did my fastest steps, my back-to-back heel clicks, and I threw in a couple of break-dance moves I learned from YouTube.

ARE YOU CRAZY?

Well, I can't say that the crowd went wild—but Mrs. Calhoun did. She was furious. She dragged me into her office and said, "Are you crazy?" about fifty times.

But when I came out of the office, the crisis was over. Everybody had gone back to what they were doing before.

Some people told me I was pretty good. Some people (Harvey) said I stunk.

Amy told me I was awesome. She said I should join the drama club with her, especially since the boys they have in there now can't dance at all. (She made sure Harvey heard her say this.)

"It's not that I can't dance," said Harvey. "I choose not to."

"Uh-huh," said Amy, and then she turned back to me and she said maybe she would start taking lessons at Debbie-Don's, too, and that would be awesome since I'd get to see her a lot more and do stuff with her outside of school and all that.

I don't know if even Origami Yoda could have given me advice this good. I mean, I didn't need to be wise . . . I needed to be a Wookiee.

CAUTION! MAD LIBR-ARIAN!

26

Harvey's Comment

Well, one thing is for sure: YOU DANCE like a Wookiee.

My Comment: First, I think it's an established fact now that Wookiees can dance. (See YouTube for proof.) Second, this really was Origami Yoda-quality advice! I have to admit, I probably would have made fun of Lance for taking dance instead of karate if he hadn't seemed so proud of it.

coooponGator! *daily deal!* Print'n'Clip'n'Save

FREE Introductory DANCE or Korean Karate Lessons at Debbie-Don's Dance Dojo!!! 모조 폼 콧수염

(Note: D.D.D. is not responsible for injuries incurred during free lessons.)

WHO IS THE NEW WEIRDEST KID IN SCHOOL?

BY KELLEN, TOMMY, AND HARVEY

After Lance's tap dance performance in the library, Rhondella said, "Well, now we know which one of you guys is the new weirdest kid in school! When Dwight left, I wasn't sure who it would be. But I think Lance just got hired."

But, of course, Amy stuck up for Lance and was like, "He's not weird. He's cool! Harvey's the weird one."

"What? What did I do?" goes Harvey, and the whole thing went on and on until we decided to take an official poll.

WHO IS THE WEIRDEST KID AT McQUARRIE?
—VOTE BELOW

I've got to vote for Murky as the weirdest guy in school. He's nice!
I like him! But he talks so weird. Everything is "total rockets" or
"pikpok" or "blimp" or "stooky." I think he thinks he is a rock star or
something. —Mike

**Murky IS a rock star! Or at least he will be. He's not weird, he's . . .
total rockets! I'm voting for Mr. Howell. Just because he isn't a kid
doesn't mean he's not the weirdest most freaked-out creepy evil
nutjob in the school/country/planet/galaxy! —Kellen**

I vote for me too pikpok pete. —Murky

**I had a really hard time deciding who to vote for. Both Tommy and
Kellen are so very, very weird. But I have to go with Tommy
because of his haircut. He looks like Ki-Adi-Mundi! —Harvey**

Tater Tot. —Sara

Maybe Kellen. He draws on EVERYTHING! —Amy

Yeah, I take back what I said about Lance. It's Kellen. No contest!
—Rhondella

Rhondella! —Remi

After Dwight, everyone else seems basically pretty normal. I guess
I'll say Brianna. Not that she's really weird, but she thinks she is
so perfect that it would be awesome if she won and was named
weirdest weirdo at the school. She'd freak. —Cassie

I MAY BE PURE EVIL... BUT I'M NOT WEIRD!

Tommy: Hmmmm . . . It looks like most people used this as a chance to insult somebody. That's not really what I had in mind—although I do like the idea of Brianna winning.

I just wondered who was the weirdest kid in school, and I guess I don't think that "weird" is an insult anymore. Not after Dwight. "Boring" maybe, but not "weird."

So I'm going to vote for Dwight!

Harvey's Comment

You completely missed the point of your OWN STUPID PoLL! Dwight can't be the weirdest kid in this school if he isn't actually IN THIS SCHOOL!

My Comment: I don't care!

All this made me wonder how Dwight was doing at his new school. He wasn't answering my e-mails. So I asked Sara, who is his next-door neighbor, to find out how he was doing after his first week in his new school.

What she found out was strange.

SARA... FINDING OUT SOMETHING STRANGE →

DWIGHT'S MOM

DWIGHT'S FIRST WEEK

BY SARA

I just got back from talking to Dwight's mom. It was a weird conversation!

Me: Hi, Mrs. Tharp!

Mrs. Tharp: Oh, hi, Sara . . .

(She said it like she wasn't that happy to see me.)

Me: Is Dwight here?

Mrs. Tharp: Yes . . . but, uh, he's upstairs doing his homework.

(This was weird because Dwight never seemed to do homework at McQuarrie. And it was also weird since she was sort of blocking the door and making it clear that I wasn't supposed to go up to see him.)

Me: Oh, I thought I'd see how he likes his new school.

Mrs. Tharp: I think he likes it a lot. I think he is really fitting in!

(Dwight? Fitting in? What????)

Me: That's great!

Mrs. Tharp: They really seem to understand how special he is. I think he's finally found the right place.

Harvey's Comment

See! I was right all along! Dwight IS much better off at a different school! Darth Paper and I did him a big favor!

My Comment: Uh, I'm not so sure . . . I don't think Mrs. Tharp really understands Dwight. And I don't think his new school does, either.

Lance found out some more stuff from a girl he takes ballet with at Debbie-Don's. She's in Dwight's class at Tippett, and her version of what Dwight's arrival was like is even stranger! Lance asked her to write it up so I could add it to this case file.

MCCALLIE

ORIGAMI YODA AND THE ORIGAMI YODAS

BY McCALLIE
(AS E-MAILED TO LANCE)

On Monday, Ms. Brendie—the guidance counselor —brought Dwight to our class. He's so cute! He looked like a little lost puppy. Right away I wanted to give him a hug, but apparently he doesn't like hugs, but that's okay because everyone is a different person and everyone likes different things and everyone is special, especially Dwight, who is very special!

Our teacher, Ms. Nelson, asked Dwight to introduce himself. But he didn't really want to say much.

MS. NELSON

"I've heard that you do something really unique, Dwight," said Ms. Nelson. "I've heard that you do or-i-gam-i."

"My mom doesn't want me to do origami at this school," mumbled Dwight. "I got into trouble at my old school."

ORIGAMI YOGA!!!

"Dwight," said Ms. Brendie, "you know I've already talked to your mom about that. You won't get into trouble for your origami here. In fact, I think it would be great if you would show everyone how to make something. Wouldn't it be great, class? I've heard Dwight knows how to make an origami yoga! Could you teach us how to make an origami yoga, Dwight?"

"It's Yoda," he mumbled.

MS. BRENDIE

Then Dwight went into this long talk about different origami Yodas and this one was folded in Japan and that one he made himself and on and on. It started to look like he was going to go on forever. Finally, Ms. Nelson said, "Well, let's all get out a piece of paper so Dwight can show us how to fold Yo-*da*."

So he did! Mine turned out lopsided, but it still looked like Yoda. Then Ms. Nelson gave us free time to draw faces on our Yodas.

When we were all done, Ms. Nelson asked Dwight to stand up again. (He had sat down.)

"Class, let's use our Yoda finger puppets to welcome Dwight to our classroom! Or as Yoda would say, 'Welcome to our classroom you are!'"

"Welcome to our classroom you are," we all said, waving our origami Yodas. Dwight looked kind of confused by the whole thing. That just made me want to hug him again.

We are so lucky to have Dwight in our class! We just love him!

And we've all been carrying around our Yodas and talking like him, too! I think we should make Origami Yoda our new classroom mascot, instead of that creepy teddy bear of Ms. Nelson's!

WE ♡ DWIGHT!

MI CHA-WA WA! THAT THING IS CREEPY!

HAVE A HUG!

YUCKKKK! They love Dwight and want to hug him???? Good grief, I'm actually starting to feel sorry for him!

My Comment: Me, too, actually.

First, because I know Dwight hates to hug people.

Second, Origami Yoda was the main thing that made Dwight Dwight. But now he's just one of thirty kids who all have their own origami Yodas.

Well, hopefully they'll start to realize that Dwight's Origami Yoda is the REAL Origami Yoda once he starts doing his Jedi-wisdom thing for them.

Meanwhile, the Fortune Wookiee was starting to show us some Jedi-quality wisdom, too.

THE FORTUNE WOOKIEE AND THE RIGHTWAYKIDZ

BY MIKE

You know how in this country we're supposed to have freedom of religion?

Well, not in my family.

In my family, you got to go to Sunday school and church every Sunday, whether you want to or not. (And our preacher takes forever.)

And you got to go to church again on Wednesday nights.

And on Friday nights I have to go to the RightWayKidz meeting.

And for some reason that I don't understand,

I have to wear uncomfortable clothes for every single one of these. I don't think it's God that wants me to wear the clothes, it's just my mom. A lot of the other kids come to the RightWayKidz meetings in T-shirts and jeans. My mom says that's disrespectful to the Lord's house.

Personally, I think it's disrespectful to be itchy in the Lord's house.

There's one good thing about all this church time, which is this girl named Cyndi. She doesn't go to our school, she's homeschooled, so church is the only time I get to see her. The bad part is she seems to dislike me just as much as the girls at school do. So it's not really worth sitting through two hours of itch just for Cyndi to say "Um . . . hi" to me.

Anyway, all that stuff is what a normal week is like. Once a month, it's even worse.

Every month the RightWayKidz hold a spaghetti dinner to raise money for our annual trip to the state RightWayKidz meeting in Richmond.

If I was rich, I would just pay for all the

RightWayKidz to go on the dumb trip without having to make twelve spaghetti dinners. Even better, I would give extra money to the bus driver to accidentally get a flat tire so we could miss the whole stupid boring meeting.

Anyway, back to the spaghetti dinners. I hate every minute of it, but the part I hate most is the cleanup. See, the RightWayKidz is for kids at our church in grades six, seven, and eight. The sixth graders greet people, tell them where to sit, and bring them garlic bread. The eighth graders cook the spaghetti sauce and the noodles and bring them to the tables on big platters.

Guess what us seventh graders get to do? Clean it all up. It's a gigantic mess. People have slopped spaghetti sauce EVERYWHERE and dropped garlic bread crumbs EVERYWHERE and spilled their drinks EVERYWHERE.

And in the kitchen, the eighth graders have made the biggest mess you've ever seen. I mean, WTS (What The Spaghetti?) are they doing in there to make that many dirty pots and pans?

I'd love to just sneak out and go home, but my mom won't let me do that, either. So I usually end up stacking chairs and putting tables away. It's not as bad as washing dishes, but it still stinks.

Well, I've had it. I can't stand it anymore. So I WAS going to ask Origami Yoda how to get out of it . . . but it turned out I couldn't ask Origami Yoda, because Dwight got kicked out of school.

I didn't really see how an origami Chewbacca was going to help me. I mean, Chewbacca is great for flying a spaceship or shooting his awesome bowcaster, but he doesn't use the Force like Yoda. How is he supposed to tell the future or give advice?

Well, I figured that since Dwight made the Fortune Wookiee, Origami Yoda may have used the Force to help him do it. I was right!

Here's what happened: I told Sara about the situation. Then she asked me which *Star Wars* movie was my favorite.

"*The Clone Wars* movie," I said, and she said, "No, it has to be one of the six episodes."

"*Episode I.*"

"One? *The Phantom Menace* is your favorite movie?" she asked.

"People always make a big deal out of me saying that. Well, I may not be free to NOT go to church, but I'm free to like whichever *Star Wars* movie I want to like, and I like *Phantom Menace*!!!"

"Ooookay," says Sara, and she counted "One" as she moved the Origami Chewbacca.

RETURN OF DARTH MAULNUT

"Which character?" she asked.

"Darth Maul!"

"D-A-R-T-H M-A-U-L," she spelled. She lifted up a triangle and said, "MMGGGGHHHRRRRR!" She does a pretty good Chewbacca impression.

"What does that mean?" I asked.

Sara got out Han Foldo.

"It means, 'There's no such thing as a lazy Wookiee, kid. A Wookiee takes the hardest job and does it well,'" said Han Foldo.

"One growl meant all that?" I asked.

"Yes," Sara said, putting both Chewie and Han in her backpack. "Now go be a Wookiee, and may the Force be with you."

That was not what I wanted to hear, but it sounded right somehow.

PASTOR
J.J.

So, we had the spaghetti dinner. The people made a mess. The eighth graders made a mess. And as usual, Pastor J.J. said, "Okay, seventh graders! It's cleanup time! Any volunteers to wash the dishes?"

Normally I would be hiding, waiting to volunteer for chair stacking or anything other than dish duty, but I decided to take the Fortune Wookiee's advice and take the hardest job.

"Me," I said.

And guess who said "me" right after me? Cyndi!

We had the greatest time. We were washing dishes for, like, two hours, and we just ended up laughing at everything. Everything was funny.

"Here's a dirty butter dish." HAHAHAHA!

GREASY
FINGER
PRINTS
WET + GROSS
SPAGHETTI
SAUCE

Everybody else had gone home. Finally, my mother came busting in and was like, "What are you doing? I've been waiting in the car for half an hour!"

Then she saw my shirt, which was smeared with spaghetti sauce and soapsuds. "Your good shirt! Honestly! Next time wear something else if you're going to do the dishes!"

Oh, yes, I will be doing the dishes next time. And the next time, and the next time . . .

And one more thing: I AM A WOOKIEE!

Harvey's Comment

Well, he does have a lot of hair, but somehow I just don't see Mike as a Wookiee. I always think of him more as an Ugnaught.

As for the "Fortune Wookiee's" advice . . . once again, Dwight has you all tricked into thinking his dumb fortune cookie sayings are some sort of wisdom. But they're really just stupid. Washing dishes for two hours, just to talk to some girl? No, thanks.

YOUR FORTUNE: ANNOYING "FRIEND" WILL MAKE A THOUSAND COMPLAINTS. 😊

43

My Comment: Well, I guess it depends on the girl. I'd wash dishes all day if it meant hanging around with Sara. I think it was great advice. Plus, sooner or later the rest of the RightWayKidz were going to beat Mike up if he kept on slacking off.

THE FORTUNE WOOKIEE REFUSES

BY KELLEN

Me: I'm thinking of growing dreadlocks.
         What does the Fortune Wookiee say?

Sara: Seriously? That's the number one
         question on your mind?

Me: Well . . .

Sara: Come back when you're ready to ask
         your real question.

Me: That was a real question!

Sara: Search your feelings. You know
         that is not the real question.

Me: Search my feelings? What are you,
         a Jedi Master all of a sudden?

Sara: Yes.

Rhondella: Now go away.

Harvey's Comment

**Dreadlocks? Kellen actually wants to look stranger
than he does now?**

My Comment: Hmmm . . . Maybe . . . Let's see the
picture, Kellen . . .

My other comment: Uh . . .

THE FORTUNE WOOKIEE AND THE LOVE-STRUCK SIXTH GRADER

BY REMI, THE LOVE-STRUCK SIXTH GRADER

okay Tommy i'll tell you my story, but DO NOT show this to Kellen . . . if you show this to Kellen i will clobber you!!!!!!!!!!!!!!!!!

Tommy's note to Tommy: Dear Me, in order to avoid being clobbered by a love-crazed sixth grade girl, do not print this section out until after Kellen is done doodling on the case file!!!!!! Sincerely, Me

my problem is that I LOVE KELLEN . . . yes it is really LOVE . . . he is so wonderful and cute and amazing! i mean he is so . . .

Tommy's note: This went on for a while. I cut it because it made me barf.

so the problem is im just this sixth grader and i only met Kellen THIS YEAR and Rhondella has known him for years and years and so obviously he knows her better and that is why he THINKS he loves her and never even notices me!

okay fine i can live with that and i will try not to hate Rhondella . . . even though she is a SNOT . . . the reason i can live with that is that i know that someday he will realize that he LOVES me much much MORE than he ever LIKED her!!!!!!

but i have to admit that it can be a giant PAIN IN MY BUTT to wait around for that day to come . . . i have been doing EVERYTHNG i can think of to make that day come faster but its impossible to even get his attention!!!

but still its okay . . . i can wait . . . but what i really really wanted was a picture to look at while i waited . . . a picture of me and Kellen TOGETHER!

i spent a couple of weeks walking around with my

cell phone ready . . . which is against the rules at school you know but i DONT care . . . i got one of him but it was from far away and it was blurry and i got in trouble but like i said i DONT CARE about the trouble i just want an unfuzzy picture with him and me both in it!

i was going to ask Origami Yoda for help . . . but then Dwight got kicked out of school! then i heard that he sent Origami Chewbacca to help and i was excited but then i heard that Sara was the one using Origami Chewbacca . . .

Tommy, i know you like Sara and that is fine . . . im sure she is nice but i cant like her because she is best friends with Rhondella who is the one making my life miserable and is also a snot . . .

well after getting in trouble for the cell phone thing i realized that i had no choice . . . i had to go to Sara and ask her to use Origami Chewbacca for me . . .

i found her in the library with Rhondella of course and i asked to speak to her privately . . . we went over to the biography area where no one EVER goes except when they absolutely have to check out a biography for a class . . .

"why dont you just ask him?" Sara asked.

actually the first thing she said was "WHAT?!?!? KELLEN?!?!? ARE YOU KIDDING?!?!?!" and i almost punched her . . . but then she settled down and said "why dont you just ask him?"

"i cant ask him!!!!!" i said . . . "then he would know and im not ready for him to know yet. it would just be embarrassing for him to find out that some sixth grader liked him while he is still all crazy for Rhondella!"

"okay so why dont you go talk to him and then i come over and take his picture?"

"you would really do that? that is so AWESOME of you. im sorry if i ever thought you were a snot like Rhondella! but if you did that he would still see the camera and wonder what you were doing . . ."

"what if i took it from across the room?" Sara asked.

"ive tried taking a picture of him that way already and its blurry . . . plus i want a close-up . . .

thats why i need the Fortune Wookiees help . . . its
impossible . . ."

"nothing is impossible for the Fortune Wookiee,"
said Sara and she got out Origami Chewbacca . . .

whats your favorite Star Wars movie? Return of
the Jedi . . . 1-2-3-4-5-6 . . . name a character . . .
Lando . . . L-A-N-D-O . . . she landed on one of the
little triangles and then she lifted it up and read
it and said:

"WAAARRGGGH!"

"uh . . . what does that mean?"

she wiggled her other puppet which was supposed
to be Han Solo: "let the Wookiee win!"

"what? let Rhondella have him??? NO WAY!!!!!" i may
have said that too loud because Rhondella looked
over and gave us one of her snotty looks . . . SNOT!

Sara giggled . . . "uh i dont think Han meant
Rhondella was a Wookiee . . . i think in this case he
meant Kellen . . . let Kellen win!"

"win what?"

"well" said Sara "you know how the school paper
always has a picture of some teacher handing some

kid a certificate or something for winning some contest? well, what if we told Kellen that he won a contest and then you handed him a certificate and i took a picture of you both? i could say, 'get closer please . . . closer! closer!'"

i admit that i squeeed after that . . . it was such a BEEYOOOTIFULLL plan!

Sara said she would figure out a way to make it all seem official to Kellen . . . she said he is pretty easy to fool. normally i wouldnt like someone saying something bad about him but this time i didnt care because i really did hope he was easy to fool this time.

my job was to get a certificate . . . i used some program on my moms computer and made a really great one! it said it was from M.A.G.I.C. Club—the McQuarrie All-Girls Comic Club—and it was a prize for him for being the best cartoonist in the school . . . WHICH HE IS!

i actually did something else too . . . at home i had this little trophy i got for winning a halloween poetry contest last year in elementary school but i always hated the trophy because it had a boy at a desk with a big pen on it! why do i want a boy trophy? And who writes with a big pen? so i was glad to get rid of it!

when i told Sara about M.A.G.I.C. she said we should make it a real club because she loves comics especially this one called ROBOT DREAMS and i think we may really do it. we told Mrs. Calhoun about our plan partly because we wanted to start the club and since shes the librarian shes going to be our club sponsor and partly because we needed her to help trick Kellen!

she said that when she was in school it was a lot harder to get pictures of boys because most kids didnt have cameras and their parents would never have let them take them to school even if they had them so you had to try to get the pictures on field trips but on field trips the boys always ran around like idiots.

she said she'd be glad to help and she wrote a little note for me to take to the office for Ms. Rabbski to read on the Morning Announcements.

so during homeroom Ms. Rabbski read this announcement over the TV: "Congratulations to Kellen Campbell winner of the M.A.G.L.C. Club's Best Cartoonist Prize for his Star Wars art . . . Kellen please report to the library after seventh period to accept your prize . . . also any girl who wants to join the M.A.G.L.C. comic book club is welcome to come too . . .

of course she got the name of our new club wrong but she got the rest right . . . four girls showed up plus me and Sara . . . and Kellen showed up too . . . he was all like "wait till i show Harvey this trophy!" (if he had said "wait till i show Rhondella" i would have punched him) and then i moved in for the photo . . . "closer . . . closer . . . smile . . ." said Sara . . .

CLICK!!!!

and i got my picture!!!!!! VERY VERY CLOSE to Kellen!!!!!!!!!!!!!!!!!!!!!!!

My Comment: Wow, I can't believe it! A girl finally likes Kellen . . . and he doesn't even know it!

CERTIFICATE

Congratulations, Kellen!

Winner of the

M.A.G.I.C. Club's

Best Cartoonist Prize

I didn't show this chapter to Kellen, and I'm not going to let Harvey see it, either, since he can't keep his mouth shut about anything ever.

But I know what Harvey would say: "Doesn't that girl know how to use the shift button? Hasn't she ever heard of an apostrophe? Enough with the exclamation points already."

DWIGHT WITHOUT ORIGAMI YODA?

BY SARA

I still haven't seen Dwight hardly at all! He's not even out in his backyard digging holes to sit in!

But I did see his mom again and I asked her how he was doing. She said almost exactly the same stuff as before, about how he was fitting in and adjusting well and all that stuff that just doesn't sound like Dwight at all.

She said to me, "I guess you know that he got in a lot of trouble at your school. Well, he hasn't been in trouble at all at Tippett! In fact, his new teacher tells me she can't get over how well behaved he is!"

And then she drops this huge bomb:

"And he's feeling so comfortable there that he isn't even taking that origami Yoda to school anymore!"

I was like, "WHAT?"

"That's a good thing! See, it was really a defense mechanism. Like a security blanket. It was a barrier between him and the real world, and now he doesn't need it anymore! I used to beg him not to take it to school, and now he doesn't even try."

I could see that she was really happy about it, so I pretended to be happy about it, too, but I don't think it's a good thing!

Harvey's Comment

Trust me, it's a good thing! And, again, I think I can take credit for helping Dwight get the help he needed!

My Comment: Uh, I think it's the other way around!

Like that thing about his teacher calling him really well behaved . . . Since when does Dwight know what "well behaved" even means? It's not that he's bad; he just doesn't know that—for example—throwing a pencil so that the point sticks into the ceiling IN THE MIDDLE OF ENGLISH CLASS is not good behavior.

This just doesn't even sound like Dwight AT ALL!

And the fact that he wasn't even bringing Origami Yoda to school really freaked me out. Something was really wrong, and I needed to find out what. I needed to talk to someone from his class myself.

To do that, I was going to have to enter the wretched hive of scum and villainy known as My Brother's Swim Team.

IF ^ORIGAMI YODA ISN'T GOING TO SCHOOL, WHAT DOES HE DO ALL DAY?

STAR THE CLONE WARS WARS

KENDYLL

ATTACK OF THE CLONES!

BY TOMMY AND KENDYLL

You know about My Brother's Swim Team, right? Well, if you don't, I'm not going to tell you. Everyone in my family is obsessed with every minor detail of My Brother's Swim Team, and I couldn't possibly give one shiny lump of Bantha dung about it myself.

But the important thing here is that a bunch of the guys on My Brother's Swim Team go to Tippett. And a while back my brother told me, "One of the guys on the team—you know, Kendyll, the hundred-meter backstroke

WHY IS IT SHINY?

guy—says that [bleep-bleep] Yoda friend of yours is in his class now."

Normally I would never speak to anyone on My Brother's Swim Team—including my brother—but this was sort of an emergency. So at the next meet—yes, I have to go to all the meets to "Support My Brother"—I asked Kendyll about Dwight while we were waiting around. (There is a LOT of waiting around at swim meets . . .)

"What's going on with Dwight? Did he stop bringing Origami Yoda to school?"

"Uh, I don't know, yeah, maybe. I guess I haven't seen him with Yoda since he gave us that really lame advice." Then he gets all uptight and starts saying, "Not that I'm ragging on Dwight! Dwight's an awesome little dude! He's great!"

After that I had trouble getting him to say anything other than how "great" Dwight is. He couldn't really say why Dwight was "great," but he wanted me to know that Dwight was

"great" and that he wasn't "ragging on him."

Finally, I got him to tell the story by promising him that I also agreed that Dwight was "great" and that I understood that he also thought Dwight was "great."

Here's basically what he said, without most of the "uh"s and "duh"s:

So, first you got to know about our teacher Ms. Nelson.

I hear that the teachers at McQuarrie are a lot less nuts than ours, so you guys probably don't have anybody like Ms. Nelson there. She seems nice, but then she has all these crazy rules for every little thing.

For example: Everything has to be a complete sentence. Always.

So if you have a question on a quiz like:

What year did Columbus discover America?

"1492?"

BEEEEP! Wrong!

The correct answer is "Columbus discovered America in 1492."

A NEW LAND FULL OF RICHES + WONDERS!

SORRY, THAT'S NOT A COMPLETE SENTENCE.

GO BACK + TRY AGAIN.

You see? It's the same exact thing! But the second one's a "complete sentence," which is apparently the most important thing in the world.

And it's not just on quizzes and tests. Like in social studies, our homework is usually answering the questions at the end of a chapter. THEY'RE FILL-IN-THE-BLANK! But can we fill in the blank? Oh no, we have to write the whole sentence again with the word filled in!

So it's like:

> The Pueblo Nation was known for its amazing cliff dwellings, which were painstakingly built into the sides of
>
> _____.

And you have to write that whole thing all over again just to put in the word "cliffs"! Yeah, you see? It's a giant waste of my time!

So we were complaining about it one day and then Tyler remembered that Caroline had told him that Dwight used to solve impossible problems at McQuarrie

SORRY
ELEVATOR
OUT OF
ORDER

CLIFF
DWELLING

by giving Yoda-style advice. This was maybe a week after Dwight got there, and so far he hadn't done anything to make us think he was really wise, but I was willing to give it a try.

So at lunch, I asked Dwight if he would help me. He looked really pleased and he got out this origami Yoda, which I have to say is really excellent. It's amazing that he can make something like that even though he's . . . uh . . . great.

"Dwight, look at tonight's homework," I said. "We're going to have to copy all those sentences out of the book and fill in the blanks. Nelson makes us write complete sentences for everything."

"I hate complete sentences," Dwight said.

"Well, uh, we were hoping your Yoda could help us figure out a way so we don't have to do it."

Dwight held up his Yoda and moved his finger a bit and made this weird voice. Again, I don't want to sound like I am making fun of Dwight, because I would never do that because he is a great little dude, but if that was supposed to be a Yoda impression, then it was a really, really bad one.

Anyway, this is what "Yoda" said:

"Complete sentences you must write. Patience and discipline you must learn."

I was like, "What? Dude, I thought you said you hated complete sentences."

"I do," said Dwight.

"You're not making any sense!" I said.

And this girl you don't know, McCallie, was like, "Kendyll . . . You're not being very nice to Dwight. He's special. I think what he said was really great!"

"Oh yeah," I said. "It was really great. Thanks, buddy!"

Then Tyler held up his own origami Yoda and said in a perfect Yoda voice: "Fast and sloppy you may write. Take off points Nelson does not."

Neil, this other guy, had been folding a piece of scrap paper into a Yoda and held it up and said, "Many abbreviations you may use. Read the whole thing Nelson does not, hmmm?"

Even McCallie did it! (And she does a surprisingly good Yoda voice!)

"Write sentences in front of TV I do. Thinking is required not."

65

So—again, not to be mean—but Dwight's Yoda gave us the lamest advice and the other Yodas all gave good advice. So I don't really see how Dwight could have solved all your problems at the old school.

But that's okay, because he's really great!

So apparently that was the last time anybody at Tippett asked Dwight for Origami Yoda's advice. They all had their own Yodas and they all thought they knew better. So now Origami Yoda isn't there and Dwight doesn't say much on his own.

I told Kendyll about how at McQuarrie it seemed like Origami Yoda was really using the Force and he was like, "Oooooookay . . ."

Harvey's Comment

OOOOOKAY

Wow, I can't believe that teachers at other schools do the complete sentences thing, too. I thought that was just Mr. Howell. He and Kendyll's teacher should get together for a HOT DATE . . . of complete-sentence writing!

OH, BABY!

THAT'S NOT A COMPLETE SENTENCE, CHUMP!

However, I'm glad to know that the kids at Tippett aren't as gullible as the kids here! Maybe I'll transfer there myself.

My Comment: Please do! And send Dwight back!

I think Dwight's mom was all wrong about that school. It doesn't sound like he's fitting in at all. He didn't stop bringing Origami Yoda because he doesn't need him; he stopped bringing Origami Yoda because the other kids didn't need him.

And did you notice how all the kids were pretending to be nice? That girl even called him "special." I think I'd rather be called "weird" than "special."

Totally unlucky that they asked Yoda about those sentences. They got a good answer, they just didn't like it.

I mean, of course Yoda was going to say that they SHOULD write the sentences. Just like he said Luke SHOULD run through the swamp and stand on his hands and eat root stew. That's how you learn discipline, patience, and Jedi mind tricks.

It actually makes a lot of sense. I wonder if I would

MMM! ROOT STEW!

become a better person if I wrote all my homework in complete sentences? Maybe I should try it. Or maybe writing all these case files is good enough.

Either way, Kendyll and his friends completely failed to learn anything, so there they are, sitting in front of the TV, writing sloppy abbreviations.

I know what Origami Yoda would say about that: "Quicker, easier is the Dark Side."

It turned out that the Fortune Wookiee's next piece of advice was also about there being no shortcuts to solving a big (pink) problem.

IF CHOOSE THE QUICK + EASY PATH YOU DO... AN AGENT OF EVIL YOU WILL BECOME...

AND FAIL SOCIAL STUDIES.

QUAVONDO

THE FORTUNE WOOKIEE AND THE BIG PINK

BY QUAVONDO

You remember my grandmother, right? She's awesome in a lot of ways.

But she has this problem with food. It's not that she's a bad cook; she can make some really delicious stuff.

The problem is the Big Pink.

The Big Pink is a meat loaf she makes. No one knows why it turns out so pink. My mother has tried to spy on Grandma in the kitchen to see what the secret ingredient is but has never found out.

At least we hope there's a secret ingredient. The alternative is that the Big Pink is pink because it hasn't actually been cooked.

The worst thing about the Big Pink is that it is served cold.

Every year at Thanksgiving, after all the other food is on the table, Grandma pulls the big platter full of Big Pink out of the refrigerator and carefully pulls off the plastic wrap.

"Here you go, Q," she said last year. "Put this on the table and no nibbling until we say grace."

Don't worry! I think. *I'm not going to eat any until I have prayed that the Big Pink won't kill me.*

One of my uncles gave it the name. He says when he was growing up there was a rock band that made an album called *Music from Big Pink*, and that was around the time that she started making the meat loaf, so he named it the Big Pink.

"You do have something to be thankful for, Q," says my uncle. "We used to have to eat it once a week. You only have to eat it at Thanksgiving."

I couldn't have eaten it every week. I would have died. It's hard enough to eat it once a year. It's so cold and jiggly and thick. And Pink. It makes you gag. One time I got a big lump of it stuck in my throat, but luckily I got it dislodged before it killed me.

Why do we have the Big Pink instead of a turkey? I asked Grandma one time—as nicely as I could. And she said, "But Q, this IS turkey!"

It turns out that it's ground-up turkey like they use to make turkey burgers with. At least with a turkey burger, you can cover it with cheese and ketchup. Plus turkey burgers are served warm and they are a lot less pink.

So that's our Thanksgiving: mashed potatoes, gravy, stuffing, and the Big Pink. The other stuff is good, but once you have a bite of the Big Pink, you lose your appetite until Christmas.

"We survived it and you'll survive it," says my mom in the car on the way to Grandma and Grandpa's every year. "You WILL eat it and you WILL NOT make a fuss about it."

I would hate to make a fuss about it, because I would hate to hurt my grandma's feelings. She's so nice about everything, and I know she's trying to be nice by making the Big Pink.

But it looks—and tastes—like Jabba's tongue. Only pinker.

Sara said the Fortune Wookiee was here to help us

with emergencies, and frankly, I consider the Coming of the Big Pink an emergency. I seriously think it could be life-threatening. So I asked if I could try using the Fortune Wookiee.

"Favorite *Star Wars* movie?"

"*Episode II.*"

"One-two," counts Sara. "Name a character."

"Jabba's tongue."

"I'll just do Jabba. J-A-B-B-A."

Sara ended up pointing to one of the little flaps inside Chewie's mouth. She lifted it up and read what was inside.

"Wuuurrrgh," said the Fortune Wookiee.

Sara put Han Foldo on her left hand.

"Good thinking, Chewie," said Han Foldo. "He says you need to be like Bom Vimdin."

"What's that?" I asked.

"Bom's not a what, he's a man," said Han. "Well, not exactly a man. He's a smuggler I used to know. A good one. Used to hang around Mos Eisley."

"A smuggler?" I asked. "I'm supposed to smuggle something into my grandma's?"

HI! I'M BOM... I WAS IN A NEW HOPE, ... BUT NO ONE REMEMBERS ME.

"No, kid, the thing about Bom was . . . he never ate meat. Total vegetarian. Tell your granny you've gone vegetarian."

"I couldn't lie to Grandma! Plus, my mother would know I was lying."

"Then don't lie, kid. Tell 'em the truth."

I looked at Sara.

"I have to tell you, Sara, this hasn't been very useful. I can't tell my grandmother the truth about the Big Pink; that's the whole point."

"No," said Sara. "You're MISSING the whole point. BECOME a vegetarian, and then you can tell them the truth."

"What?"

"Look, you've got, like, three weeks until Thanksgiving. Stop eating meat now and your parents won't suspect a thing. Keep it up through Thanksgiving and you'll be home free."

"But I like to eat meat."

"Yeah, I know," said Sara. "I've seen the junk you wolf down in the cafeteria. Rib-B-Qs and double cheese-burgers and pepperoni rolls. The other day you ate three

PUDDLE O' GREASE

73

CORNDOG1   CORNDOG2   CORDOG3

corn dogs! Really? Do you know how many nitrites are in those things?"

"Nitrites?"

"Geez, don't you pay any attention to what you eat? Believe me, going veg is going to be the best thing that ever happened to you. You might even live till high school."

CHEETOS

"All I care about is living past Thanksgiving," I said.

"All right, then you've got to start now," she said. "And one more thing: Lay off the Cheetos, too. They're a sometimes food."

(HARD TO DRAW!)

Well, Sara was a bit obnoxious about all of that. But I realized that she and Han and Chewie were right.

At lunch I had one last round of meat—two double cheeseburgers—and when I got home that night I told my mother I'd decided to go vegetarian. There was a certain amount of fuss about it, and I wound up eating a lot of rice and bread for the next three weeks. I had to keep it up at school, too, so my sister wouldn't catch me eating meat. But rice and bread is a whole lot better than the Big Pink.

By the time Thanksgiving rolled around, my family was pretty used to me being a vegetarian. My mom even

OH THESE @N #
KIDS!! WHAT
#!@# NEXT?

mentioned it to Grandma on the phone before we went.
I don't know what Grandma said—probably a cuss word,
if I know Grandma—but Mom said, "It's probably just a
phase. He'll give it up soon."

Yeah, you bet I'll give it up soon! The day AFTER
Thanksgiving.

So all I had to do was show up and watch as Grandpa cut
huge slices of Big Pink for everyone else's plate. I pigged
out on mashed potatoes, stuffing, and cranberry sauce. I
couldn't eat the gravy—which is made with chicken broth
or something—but that was a small price to pay.

I was watching my uncle try to choke down a big
chunk of it, and he looked up and saw me. I think he knew
what I was doing, but he didn't tell on me. I think he may
be a vegetarian by next Thanksgiving, too.

At the end of the meal, I was able to look Grandma in
the eye and thank her for a delicious meal.

"Oh, poor Q, missing out on the meat loaf. And you
won't be able to have my ham aspic at Christmas, either,
I guess."

I had forgotten about the ham aspic. It's like Jell-O
with pig in it.

It looks like I'm going to stay vegetarian at least through Christmas.

Bom Vimdin? I have to give Dwight credit—he knows his _Star Wars_ better than I thought.

And this advice was great! I don't care about what Quavondo eats at his grandmother's house, but it sure is nice not having to watch him go carnivore at lunch anymore.

My Comment: For once, Harvey and I agree! This piece of Fortune Wookiee advice was great. Very much like Origami Yoda's advice back in the old days. If he keeps it up, I think we're going to have some serious thinking to do about how Dwight could have created a fortune teller that really, actually works even though Dwight isn't there to operate it. That seems like a lot, even for the Force . . .

I CAN EAT 4 CORN DOGS AT A TIME!

TRY THAT, JEDI SCUM!

THE FRAMING OF ORIGAMI YODA

BY TOMMY

On the day after Thanksgiving, I decided to go see Dwight myself. I knew we would both be out of school, and I figured I might get a chance to talk to him and finally find out what was going on. Maybe I'd even get a chance to talk to Origami Yoda.

It was seriously cold out and I had to ride my bike, which is a terrible combination because the parts of you that are under your coat get all sweaty, but your hands and face freeze up and your lungs get all weird.

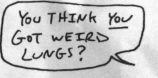

YOU THINK YOU GOT WEIRD LUNGS?

WHEEZE WHEEZE WHEEZE

The last time I had ridden to Dwight's house, it had only been a tiny bit chilly. That was about three weeks ago. After the whole Darth Paper thing. It was hard to believe how much things had changed since then.

I had to wait forever to get across Route 24. Lots of traffic. Everybody was headed to town for Black Friday, like my parents.

Finally I got to Cascade Drive and rode past Sara's house. Nobody home. They had probably gone shopping, too.

Dwight's house was next, and his mom's car was gone. I rang the bell and knocked, but nobody answered.

Normally I don't peek in windows, but since I had come all that way, I looked through one of the windows that are on each side of the door.

Dwight was standing right there!

"Dwight, it's me, Tommy. Open the door!"

He shook his head no.

"What? Dude, let me in!"

He walked toward the door and I lost sight of him.

Then the doggie door opened up. I could only see his hand sticking out.

"I'm not allowed to unlock the door," he said.

"Why not?"

"My mom's not home. She's working an extra job now."

An extra job? I had wondered how Dwight's mom could afford to send him to Tippett Academy. I've heard it's really expensive.

"Uh, can you at least open a window so we can talk normally?"

"No, they're nailed shut."

"Why are they nailed shut?"

"So I don't fall out."

I was about to ask him why he would fall out a window when I realized I might freeze to death before I found out. My sweat was turning into sweatsicles under my coat.

"Is there a rule against me crawling through the doggie door?"

ARM
PIT
XRAY

"Well, I'm not supposed to let anyone in."

"You're not letting me in, I'm coming in on my own!"

I took off my coat and shoved it through. Then I squeezed through, too. Luckily, the doggie door was for a fairly big dog.

"Do you have a dog?" I asked Dwight.

"Not anymore," said Dwight. "My dad took him."

"Oh." I had never heard Dwight mention his dad before. I didn't even know he had one. Well, I knew he had one. Anyway . . .

"Well . . . how are you?" I asked.

"Fine."

Long pause.

"Uh, you got any neat origami to show me?"

"Not really."

Long pause.

"Thanks for sending the Fortune Wookiee. I'm keeping a case file about it. Do you want to read it?"

"I don't know what you mean."

FORTUNE WOOKIEE

"A case file, dude! Like the ones for Origami Yoda and Darth Paper! I'm making one for the Fortune Wookiee!"

"Uh, okay."

Well, this conversation was going nowhere at all! But it's always been hard to talk to Dwight. Origami Yoda is the one that usually makes more sense.

"Can I see Origami Yoda?"

"Okay, I guess."

We went into his bedroom. Still the most boring bedroom in the world, but now even more boring because there weren't any piles of origami. It looked like it was from a catalog or something. A lame catalog.

But there was something new. On the wall—next to that stupid plastic anchor that had probably been hanging there since Dwight was two—was a picture frame.

And there, under the glass, was Origami Yoda!

That was creepy. The whole room was creepy!

No human being could ever keep their room this neat. Only someone's mother could or would put absolutely everything away, including Origami Yoda!

The only thing that was not put away was a book, and not one of Dwight's usual science fiction books, but, like, a school history book.

He started reading the book! While I was standing right there.

"Uh, Dwight, we need to talk," I said.

I won't even bother to write down our whole conversation—because it was boring.

Conversations with Dwight never used to be boring. Weird, maybe. Annoying, sometimes. Funny, usually. But not boring!

I asked Dwight if he was having a problem at his new school.

No.

Did he like the new kids?

Yes.

Were they nice to him?

Yes.

How about the teachers?

Yes.

Was he getting in any trouble?

No.

Was he folding origami?

No. He said his mother really wanted him to start focusing on his schoolwork.

Was he getting good grades?

All A's so far.

So, no problems?

No.

Did he think he'd come back to McQuarrie when his suspension was over or stay at Tippett?

Stay.

What? Why?

Then he finally said something.

"It's kind of nice not getting in trouble and not getting made fun of and not battling Harvey or somebody all the time. It makes life a lot easier."

Compared to some of the wacky conversations

I've had with Dwight in the past—like when he only said "purple" or talked about squirrel power or explained what was wrong with his belly button—this was a lot like talking to a normal person. But, like I said, it was also boring except for that last part, which was kind of sad.

So I saw that Dwight was definitely different, but I had no idea what to do about it. And I wasn't sure I SHOULD do anything about it, since Dwight himself said things were better than they used to be. Maybe things really WERE better for Dwight this way. They didn't seem better to me, but why should I interfere?

Of course, I knew what to do when I had a tough decision like that to make.

"Dwight, can I ask Origami Yoda about all this?"

"Uh, he's really hard to get out of the frame," said Dwight.

"What is he doing in a frame, anyway? Why aren't you taking him to school?"

"I don't need him at school," said Dwight. "Things are just easier at Tippett."

And that was about all I got out of him. He didn't seem to be interested in any of the stuff I had to tell him about what was going on at McQuarrie. He didn't even want to talk about *Star Wars*! I got my coat and unlocked the front door so I wouldn't have to crawl back out.

"Bye, Dwight!" I called.

He locked the door behind me.

Harvey's Comment

As usual, I get the blame.

click

My Comment: Actually, I've been starting to think you might be right about the new school, Harvey. Maybe it is what he needed. Maybe it's helping him learn how to not be the weirdest kid in the whole school. Maybe he's learned to control the weirdness so that he can fit in, and he seems to like fitting in. Maybe they've fixed him.

CAROLINE

NORMALNESS

BY TOMMY AND CAROLINE

I got an e-mail from Caroline the next day. Caroline is that girl who Dwight likes a lot—almost like a girlfriend. And the crazy thing is that she likes him, too! I always suspected that Dwight got himself sent to Tippett just because Caroline goes there.

Anyway, she wrote:

Tommy—

Dwight got in huge trouble with his mom for letting you in yesterday. He isn't allowed to meet me at Wendy's tonight for our weekly non-date.

But I'm glad you went to see him. I'm worried sick about him.

It's so frustrating because I don't get to see him very much. See, the grades are a lot more separate here at Tippett than they are at McQuarrie. Some days I barely see him at all, which stinks.

But what I do see of him stinks even worse, because he's less and less like Dwight. He's just ... well, kind of boring. He never brings new origami to school or makes his crazy jokes or any of that stuff. He doesn't even say "purple" anymore.

The last time we went to Wendy's, you know what he got? A SALAD! Dwight Tharp ordered a salad! And the Kids' Meals had Scooby toys in them. He picked a salad over a Scooby toy? That's not Dwight!

What did you think? Did you think he was acting weird, too? And by acting weird, I mean acting "normal," which is weird for Dwight ... and no fun for me.

—Caroline

SALAD
-OR-
RACIN'
VELMA?

So I wrote back and told her that I had been worried about him, too. But I also told her that he seemed to be happy, or at least not miserable.

Here are our e-mails:

Yes, he was acting kind of normal. Maybe getting kicked out of school sort of made him realize how weird he was, and now he's finally figured out how to be normal. Isn't that a good thing?

—Tommy

For the most interesting person I've ever met to suddenly become the most boring person I've ever met? Uh, no, that's not a good thing.

He may SAY he's happy, but I don't think he REALLY is. If you knew what things are like at school, I think you would agree with me.

—Caroline

Well, I guess I have no idea what it's like . . . so why don't YOU write a chapter for my case file that shows me what things are like at school, and maybe it will help us figure out what to do to help Dwight—if he really needs help.

—Tommy

YES I will write a chapter and YES he really does need help and YES I will prove it to you! And I really hope we can figure out how to help him . . .
—Caroline

Harvey's Comment

Let me get this straight: Dwight is no longer getting in trouble and no longer making a fool of himself on a daily basis. So you two are going to "help" him start getting in trouble and making a fool of himself again?

My Comment: Well, yeah, I kind of agree with you. If Tippett has "fixed" Dwight, then I don't see why we should mess with him. If he wants to be normal, then maybe we should let him be.

Meanwhile, we've got plenty of our own problems here at McQuarrie. This next story shows that maybe the Fortune Wookiee isn't powerful enough to save us from disaster after all . . .

DWIGHT   NOT DWIGHT!

SALAD

39¢

THE FORTUNE WOOKIEE AND THE FLIGHT OF THE MILLENNIUM RUG-BONI

BY MURKY

BEFORE I DID IT: I was at Valley View Mall with Lance + Ben + unfortunately my pikpok sister Karina too

we were gonna look at the xmas decorations but that took about fifteen milliseconds and we were so bored we were actually walking down that long hall that comes off of Sears and goes out the back to where the Sears tire changing place is

I had never actually walked down there before but they have a couple of vending machines

and when we got past the vending machines we saw something we couldnt believe . . .

it was the Rug-Boni!!!!!!!!

"stooky!!!" I shouted. in case you dont know what a Rug-Boni is do you know what a ZAMboni is? a Zamboni is this jacked-up thing they drive around on the ice at a hockey game to make the ice icier or something. Ben told me about it. he watches hockey on TV and used to go see the Roanoke hockey team play before they stopped

well a Rug-Boni is like a Zamboni but for carpets instead of ice!

its like a vacuum cleaner that you ride on!!!!!

the only reason I know its called a Rug-Boni by the way is that it says RUG-BONI right on the side of it! draw a picture of it Kellen!

Ive seen the dude using it to vacuum those super-long rugs that go down the middle of the mall floor but I thought they locked it

91

PLASTIC DINOSAURS

up somewhere when he was done. instead it was just sitting there plugged into the wall. it must have a rechargeable battery or something

Me: "plastic dinosaurs!!!! we could totally take a ride on this thing!"

Lance: "do it!"

Ben: "yeah! that would be bolt!"

Karina: "yeah! do it!"

when I heard the way Karina said "yeah" I realized she was hoping I would do it so she could tell Mom and get me in huge trouble for the fifty millionth time

our parents are 100 percent serious about following the rules + they would think riding a Rug-Boni was a major felony

Me: "one of you guys want to do it?"

Ben: "no thanks"

Lance: "ooh I want to man but I dont want to get busted"

Me: "whos going to bust you? its not like you have an annoying sister watching everything you do"

Lance: "Yeah but Randy might be"

Randy is one of the mall cops. he stops and talks to kids all the time:

"Hi kids do you have an adult with you today? You know kids arent allowed to walk around the mall without an adult after seven pm right?"

"YEAH RANDY WE KNOW BUT ITS ONLY 5:30 YOU IDIOT!" is what we do not say to him

anyway nobody would ride the Rug-Boni

I didnt say any more about it but . . . I knew I had to do it

and I knew I COULD do it cuz I knew I could figure out a way to do it without getting busted by Randy or anybody!

thank Jabba one of Karinas friends came by and they went into Hot Topic together and me + Lance + Ben went down to the food court to get Chinese food which is better at the mall than at the Chinese buffet but is pretty pikpok expensive at the mall

Ben wanted to go with Karina because he likes the friend but he wussed out and came with us to Mongolian Express

BEN = WUSS

MEGAN? OR MEGHAN?

Me: "Lance stop waving at the cat statue"

Lance: "but its waving at me!" Lance can be pretty embarrassing sometimes

After we got through the line and sat down I made my announcement

Me: "Im going to ride the Rug-Boni"

Lance: "bolt!"

Ben: "right now?"

Me: "no not right now. Im going to think about it. Im going to do it smart. this is totally a stealth mission so Im going to study things and figure out how to do it without getting busted then Im going to come in here and do it solo"

Lance: "without us?"

Me: "thats what 'solo' means"

Ben: "how will we know you really did it?"

Me: "you wont believe me?"

Ben + Lance: "NO!"

Ben: "it would be like the time you said you went on the roof of the school"

NOTE: NO MURKY

SCHOOL ROOF

Me: "I did!"

Lance: "uh-huh the only problem with that is . . ."

this narnar goes on and on and on cuz they refuse to believe I went on the roof of the school—well it wasnt exactly ON the roof but thats totally beside the pikpok point!!!!!!!!!!

Me: "fine!!!!!!!!!! I'll set up my phone to take a video of me doing it. Will you believe that?"

Ben: "I'll believe it when I see it"

Lance: "I dont think you should do it. Randy will get you"

Me: "no he wont"

Lance: "yes he will or one of the other ones"

Me: "Im telling you they wont"

Lance: "man I wish Origami Yoda was still around to talk you out of it. hey maybe you should ask Saras Fortune Wookiee first"

Me: "thats actually a good idea! Chewbacca

knows how to fly anything . . . even a Rug-Boni!!"

so the next day at school I went into the library and found Sara + everybody and I asked her to ask the Fortune Wookiee and we did all that whats-your-favorite-movie stuff and she moved it back and forth and then lifted up a flap of paper and went "Wwwwrhhh wwwwwhhhhh"

Me: "whats that mean?"

Sara talking through a Han Solo puppet: "he said 'only a great pilot can fly a Rug-Boni'"

Harvey: "really? I didnt know that Wookiees had a word for Rug-Boni—'wwwwwhhhhh' means 'Rug-Boni' in Shyriiwook?? I'll have to remember that"

[that guy is SO annoying!!!!!!!! how do they stand him????] A: WE CAN'T!!

Me: "dont worry its basically like riding a lawn mower and I used one of them last summer"

96

Sara/Han Foldo: "flying a Rug-Boni aint like mowing crops kid"

Harvey: "its 'dusting' crops not 'mowing' crops!"

Tommy: "yeah we know!! its a joke dude! she changed the quote to make a joke"

Harvey: "so you finally admit its just a joke! I was beginning to think it was really the Force but if you say its just a joke . . ."

[We left! I cant stand listening to that kid + his narnar!!!]

Me: "you satisfied Lance?"

Lance: "no I still wish Origami Yoda was here because I think he'd have tried harder to stop you"

AFTER I DID IT:

Me: "WAAAAHHHHHH!!!!!!!!!"

now I wish Origami Yoda had been there to stop me too

TOTAL FISHMASTER DISASTER!!!!!!!

97

things went well at first

I got my mom to drop me off at the mall on a Monday afternoon. usually nobody goes on a Monday and thats how it was this time. hardly anybody around and nobody at all in that hallway where they keep the Rug-Boni. just the way I wanted it!

but I was playing it smart so I didnt just run over there and jump on it. I sat on a bench across the main part of the mall and waited . . . Randy + another guard walked by and went off toward the food court

I figured I would have plenty of time before they came by again as long as I moved quickly so I walked past a trash can and set my cell phone on the edge of it then I checked the screen and it gave me a great view of the hallway down to the vending machines so I hit record

I walked super-fast down to the Rug-Boni and unplugged it from the wall and got on. it was bigger than a mower actually

I turned on the power switch and the vacuum started up. it seemed loud but not too loud. they must make it so it doesnt bother customers

the controls looked pretty simple not like mower controls though

I pushed a switch forward and off I went and it wasnt quite as stooky as I had expected. it really WAS like riding a mower but even slower. Id probably have just gotten off if I didnt need to ride it out into the hall for the camera so I kept going and when I got up next to the vending machines I turned right so Id go out in the middle of the hall and make a big circle on the video

BUT I DIDNT GO RIGHT!!!!!!!!!!!!!!!!!!!!!!!

when I turned the wheel right the Rug-Boni didnt turn the way a mower does!!! instead of the front wheels turning the BACK wheels turned. They went way out on the left side and CRACK!!! right into the Coke machine!!!!!!!!!!!!!!!!

MOWER

RUGBONI

 that light-up plastic panel on the front of the machine was cracked and the bottom of it didnt light up anymore . . .

I took off! right out the exit and came out at the tire place and some tire guys were around but none of them noticed me so I just kept speed-walking around the outside of the mall. it was cold out but I wasnt going to go back inside I was just going to wait outside JCPenney for my mom to pick me up

I was freaking out a bit but I didnt see any reason why I was going to get into trouble so I just needed to calm down before Mom got there . . .

Then I remembered the cell phone!!!!!!!!
PIKPOK PETE!!!!!!!!!!!!

Rest of the story: Randy found my cell phone first and showed my parents the movie of me crashing the Rug-Boni

MONSTERLY MASSIVE TROUBLE!!!!!

1) $250 to fix the Coke machine

2) Im not allowed in the mall anymore

3) not that I could go anyway since Im
   grounded for the rest of the year—the
   SCHOOL year!—and since we live nowhere
   being grounded means nothing to do ever

4) MY LIFE = UNSTOOKY!!!!!!!!!!!

Harvey's Comment

This is the dumbest thing I've ever read in my whole
life, and I'm not even talking about all the "pikpok"s
and the lack of punctuation.

I'm talking about someone wanting to ride on a
vacuum cleaner. Huh? Why?

But this case file does prove something. It proves
that the Fortune Wookiee's fortunes are lame.

If it could REALLY tell Murky's fortune, it would
have said, "Watch out for the Coke machine, idiot!"

Actually, I think I know the reason the Fortune
Wookiee didn't give a stronger warning. Because
stealing a Rug-Boni is exactly the sort of thing
Dwight would do himself.

And would someone please make a Murky-to-English Dictionary so we can figure out what he's talking about?

My Comment: You know, I can see Dwight trying to ride the Rug-Boni, too!

But I don't think it's fair to blame this on Dwight/the Fortune Wookiee not giving a stronger warning. It WAS a clear warning; Murky just ignored it.

As for the Murky-to-English Dictionary... great idea!

MURKY-TO-ENGLISH DICTIONARY

BY TOMMY, KELLEN, LANCE, AND MURKY

bolt – awesome

Jell-O – as awesome as Jell-O

massively – very

monsterly – very very

narnar – rude, boring, or just unawesome conversation

pikpok – not awesome

pikpok Pete! – what to say when something is not awesome

plastic dinosaurs! – what to say when something is awesome

stooky (adjective) – awesome

stooky (noun) – what you call an awesome
person other than "dude"

stookiness – awesomeness

total rockets – awesome in every way

Harvey's Comment

So basically, he's just saying "awesome" all the
time? Good grief...

My Comment: NO, he's not saying "awesome" all the
time, that's the whole point! It gets annoying when
people just say "awesome" all the time. Plus, someone
will see a cupcake and they'll say "awesome," then
they'll see a meteor blow up the moon and they'll say
"awesome." The word is becoming meaningless. (And
annoying.)

Murky is creating a new language to deal with all
the different levels of awesomeness.

I SPEAK
3 MILLION
LANGUAGES.
BUT I DON'T
HAVE A BEEP
CLUE WHAT
MURKY'S TALKING
ABOUT!

'TIS BETTER TO GIVE THAN TO RECEIVE

BY KELLEN

Me: Sara, I really, really need to ask the Fortune Wookiee a question.

Sara: Great. The Fortune Wookiee is ready for your important question.

Me: What am I getting for Christmas?

Sara: ARGGH! Forget it!

Me: But seriously, I really need to know. See, I want to buy this game for PlayStation, but I'm hoping my parents are going to get me the new Xbox for Christmas. And if I get that, I won't need the PlayStation game, so—

Sara:	Listen, Greedo, why don't you take that money and buy someone else a present for once?
Me:	Is that Chewie's advice?
Sara:	No, it's anybody's advice. Anybody —even Jabba the Hutt—would tell you to stop thinking about yourself for ten minutes and get something for somebody else!
Me:	Okay, okay.
Sara:	It's better to give than to receive. Ever heard of that?
Me:	I said okay!

Harvey's Comment

→ Yep, Tommy's got himself a real nice girlfriend there. She's just so sweet and wuvable!

My Comment: It's not her fault that Kellen's a greedy pig! And, you have to admit, that Greedo joke was pretty funny.

SNOWTROOPER

THE FORTUNE WOOKIEE AND THE SNOT TROOPER

BY TOMMY

What happened with me and the Fortune Wookiee is in a way almost weirder than anything that happened with Origami Yoda.

It was weird because Origami Yoda always helped me win. But with the Fortune Wookiee, I had already won and then the Fortune Wookiee made me lose. Really weird.

The thing is, I wasn't planning on asking the Fortune Wookiee anything. I mean, things were going pretty good for me. Sara and I were hanging around together every chance we got, and it was great.

But then one morning in the library, Sara told me it was time for me to get my fortune told by the Fortune Wookiee.

"What are you talking about?" I said. "I don't even have a question."

"That doesn't matter, because the Fortune Wookiee told me he has an answer."

"He tells you things?"

"Well, Han Foldo was the one who told me, but anyway, what's your favorite *Star Wars* movie?"

BEEP!

And we went through the whole routine again, except this time I said R2-D2, who really is my favorite character. (Except for maybe Yoda.)

So Sara got to the right flap and read it and the Fortune Wookiee went, "MRRRGH."

Then Han Foldo said, "Apologize? Why should he apologize?"

And the Fortune Wookiee said, "MRRRRRRRGH!"

"Oh, come on," said Han Foldo. "Harvey had it coming."

"MRRRRRRRRRRRRRGH!"

"All right, all right!" Then Han Foldo turned to look at me. "Chewie says you have to apologize."

"For what?" I asked.

"For what?" gasped Sara. "For the whole snot trooper thing! Duh!"

The snot trooper thing had happened the day before, when Mr. Good Clean Fun came and did his Holiday Health and Hygiene Hoedown. He did a big thing about not sneezing into your hand when you have a cold.

"Germs don't make good presents!"

Then he and his monkey puppet, Soapy, demonstrated how to use a Kleenex.

Well, the ironic thing is that while we were watching all this, I had to blow my nose for real!

I got a cold from my dumb twin cousins over Thanksgiving, and it lasted for two weeks! That's what happens when you have to sit at

109

the kids' table with a couple of four-year-olds! They don't know how to sneeze into their elbows; they just sneeze right on the turkey or whatever is in front of them. (My stupid brother, who is only three years older, gets to sit at the adult table!!)

Anyway, my nose was running, and of course since we're in the gym for the assembly there are no tissues anywhere—except the one Mr. Good Clean Fun and Soapy are using.

I tried sniffling, but the mucus was past the point of no return. I started to get worried that people could see it hanging out my nose! I was pretty tempted to ask Mr. Good Clean Fun if I could borrow Soapy's used tissue when I saw that Harvey had been very, very quietly folding origami instead of paying attention.

"Hey, can I see it?" I whispered.

He held it up. It was a pretty good snowtrooper, but of course I wasn't going to tell him that.

Instead I took it and . . . . well, let's just say I didn't need a Kleenex anymore.

Kellen was watching all this and he let out a big laugh-snort.

I handed the snowtrooper back to Harvey. The look on his face was awesome! It felt great to finally score one on Harvey!

Then he flipped out. I should have known he would flip out, but I didn't see it coming until all of a sudden he's yelling and EVERYBODY in the whole school is looking at us and Mr. Good Clean Fun and Soapy have stopped singing "We Wish You a Merry Mucus" and every teacher in the gym is trying to get to us.

And guess who got there first? Our mean old sixth grade homeroom teacher, Mr. Howell.

"OUT! All three of you!" he roared.

Harvey just kept on yelling as Howell dragged us out of the gym. Then HE started yelling at us before we got through the doors. The whole way Kellen was saying, "I didn't do anything!" But Howell just out-yelled him.

"I see you haven't learned one thing about not acting like animals since you were in my class! That was a new level of embarrassment! What on earth were you hardheads doing, anyway?"

"Tommy just blew his nose on my snowtrooper!"

"Correction," whispered Kellen. "Snot trooper."

"SHUT UP," I hissed. If Kellen made me laugh, Howell would explode all over again.

"Well, that's the sort of disgusting behavior I've come to expect from you, Tommy. But Harvey, you shouldn't have been messing around with origami during an assembly or anywhere else but the library. Oh, yes, I know about Ms. Rabbski's rule. Apparently you have forgotten about it. Well, I'm sure she'll be happy to remind you. I almost wish I could deal with you myself, but I have a feeling Ms. Rabbski has a lot she would like to say about this."

"But I—" started Kellen.

"RABBSKI'S OFFICE! NOW!" howled Howell.

We got to the office before Rabbski, so we had to sit in there and wait.

"Nice going!" I said.

And Harvey goes, "Me? You did it!"

"Yeah, I played a LITTLE joke. You're the one that acted like a BIG baby, made us all look like idiots, and got us in trouble!"

"Yeah," said Kellen, "and I didn't even—"

The door opened.

"I'm so sorry to keep you waiting," said Rabbski. "I've been busy trying to apologize for your completely unacceptable behavior to Mr. Good Clean Fun."

The calm tone in her voice was scarier than Howell's yelling.

"Now, do you have any sort of feeble excuses to offer?"

When Ms. Rabbski found out what started the whole thing, she told Harvey, "Normally,

I would confiscate your origami, but in this case I'll ask you to deposit it directly in the trash."

"Oh, but that's the best one I've—" started Harvey.

"IT'S TRASH NOW!" Rabbski screeched. Then she lectured us awhile, made us scrub our hands with sanitizer, and finally sent us to I.S.S. for the rest of the day, and you know what that means: a note home to my parents. UGH!

What I was planning to do when I saw Harvey the next day was tell him what a jerk he is. If he had just rolled with it, none of us would be in trouble!

Apologizing was the *last* thing on my mind.

"Oh, come on," said Sara. "If Harvey had blown his nose on Dwight's Origami Yoda, you guys would have thrown a fit!"

"Yeah, but—"

"No! Harvey worked hard on making something and you blew snot all over it. End of story."

"MMRRRRGH!" added the Fortune Wookiee.

Wow. I realized they were totally right. Instead of me scoring a big victory against Harvey, it was more like that part in ESB where Luke goes in the swamp cave and he thinks he beats Dream Vader, but then he finds out he was Dream Vader all along.

"I feel like a total jerk," I told Sara.

"Well, here comes Harvey. You know what to do."

So I did it.

Harvey's Comment

Apology NOT accepted!

ME NEITHER! YOU ⚡#@!°% KIDS RUINED MERRY #! ⚡⚡@ MUCUS!!!

THE NON-ATTACK OF THE SPIDERS

BY AMY

I was down at the public library the other day. The one on Peter's Creek Road near the putt-putt. And I saw my poster hanging up!

It was from that Library Week poster contest they have at school every year. Remember when we all made posters last month about library stuff and then they hung them up in the hall and people were supposed to vote on them? I got second place, behind that eighth grader Colby who made that poster of Edward from *Twilight*. So I looked at my poster and Colby's poster—not to brag, but I have to say that

GLITTER

COLBY

mine was better. It just didn't have a pound of glitter like Colby's.

Anyway, they had posters from some other schools, too, and they even had ones from Tippett Academy. I used my mom's cell phone to take a picture of the first-place winner:

Yeah, it's Dwight's poster! Can you believe it? It's so . . . boring.

I mean, you remember the one he made at our school last year, right? With the spiders?

Now that poster rocked! It totally would have won if it hadn't been disqualified.

So what I'm wondering is . . . what is up with Dwight? Has Tippett made him boring?

Harvey's Comment

It's weird that Dwight doing something not-weird is weird. And what's even more weird is that I feel weird about it.

I know I always said that I wished Dwight would act normal . . . but that's just Too normal!

My Comment: Totally agree!

And you know what else is weird? Why would the kids at Tippett vote for that lousy poster? Either the other posters really, really, really stunk OR they voted for him out of pity or something.

CASSIE

THE FORTUNE WOOKiEE AND THE TWIST

BY CASSiE

Life is so unfair!!!

I finally got the lead role in a play. After being Girl #3 in *Outside Looking In* and the dumb late Rabbit in *Wonderland the Musical*, I finally had a good part. I was going to be Olivia in *Olivia Twist.*

Olivia Twist is just *Oliver Twist* but with a girl pathetic orphan instead of a boy pathetic orphan. Why? Because the only boy who tried out for the play was Harvey, who is, like, six feet tall all of a sudden. (Plus, he can't act.)

So Mrs. Hardaway made him the bad guy and just changed every "he" to a "she" in our scripts.

MRS. HARDAWAY

LES MIZ!

And some of the other characters had to change, too. Like the Artful Dodger is still the Artful Dodger, but it's played by Amy. And Brianna is playing the old dude who saves Oliver, so she's going to be an old lady. (She has to wear a gray wig, which is funny because she is so show-offy about her hair all the time and now she looks like Martha Washington or something.)

But actually none of that stuff is going to happen. Because just a few days after we got started, Mrs. Hardaway—the chorus teacher who runs the drama club and directs the plays—told us we would have to "wait and see" about the play until after winter break. She said there was a good chance we wouldn't be able to do it, so there was no need for us to rehearse.

She wouldn't tell us why and asked us not to ask her about it anymore. She said she was very upset about it, but couldn't say anything. She said we would find out what we needed to know in January. It was all very mysterious, which is what made me think of Dwight and Origami Yoda.

See, Dwight likes to do this awful Sherlock Holmes

accent and play detective with Origami Yoda's help. The first time he did it, he actually caught me doing something bad but helped me fix it. The second time he solved a different mystery for us that saved our last play.

But this time he wasn't around to help us save the play, so I didn't know what to do.

I knew that Sara was helping people with her Fortune Wookiee, but I really didn't see how Chewbacca was going to solve a mystery like this. But since I ride the bus with Sara, I ended up telling her all about it on the way to school.

"Why don't we try it and see if it works?" she said. "It's been working good so far."

So we did the whole cootie catcher thing and ended up on one of the flaps. She lifted it up and looked underneath.

"That's weird," she said. "It usually tells me what Chewbacca would say, but all it says is 'Nien Nunb.' That doesn't sound like a Chewbacca line."

"No," I told her, "Nien Nunb is a character from *Return of the Jedi*. He's the guy who replaces Chewbacca when Lando flies the Millennium Falcon."

NIEN NUNB

Sara held up her origami Han Solo, but then said in her normal voice, "Do you really want to talk to Han Foldo, or can I just tell you what I think?"

"Yeah, just tell me."

"Well," she said, "I think the Fortune Wookiee showed me Nien Nunb because it wants me to replace Dwight and be the detective."

"You're going to solve the mystery yourself?"

"Elementary, my dear Cassie," she said in a British accent. But then she laughed, so I knew she wasn't crazy like Dwight.

So that afternoon on the way home from school, she told me what she had found out.

"I went to see Mrs. Hardaway. As I approached her room, I heard a hammering followed by a horrible screeching sound. Fearing that she was being murdered, I raced to the scene."

Sara was saying all this in a Sherlock Holmes voice, just like Dwight used to! Right there on the bus. It was totally embarrassing!

"Upon entering the chorus room, I found Mrs.

123

SCREECH!

BANG

Hardaway quite alive. The screeching sound had come from a roll of packing tape. Mrs. Hardaway had torn off a long piece and was closing up a cardboard box.

"The hammering? That, too, was easily explained. An electrician was on the other side of the room installing one of those strips of electrical outlets.

"I told Mrs. Hardaway that I had been inspired by seeing *Wonderland the Musical* and wanted to join the drama group."

"Is that true?" I asked Sara.

"Er, no. In this case I decided honesty was not the best policy. I told her I wanted to be part of *Olivia Twist*, even if I was just a random orphan or something without any lines.

"She told me basically the same thing she told you and wouldn't say anything else. It was a bit hard to talk with the hammering and all, so I left."

"So you didn't find out anything?" I asked.

"On the contrary!" Sara said. "I found out everything."

"What?"

"Why, it's elementary, my dear Cassie . . ."

<<GROAN>>

". . . why would a chorus room need a bunch of electrical outlets?"

"Uh . . ."

"Exactly. It doesn't. Hardaway hinted at changes coming after winter break. It is my belief that after break, when the new semester begins, that room will no longer be a chorus room. Recall the cardboard box! Hardaway was packing her things!"

"Well, that's weird, but I don't see why she should cancel the play just because she's changing rooms."

"Aha! You forget a crucial element, Dr. Cassie."

"What?"

"The packing tape! If Hardaway was merely moving her chorus class to another classroom, she would have no need of packing tape; she would pile boxes on a cart and wheel it down the hall. No, Cassie, it is my belief that neither the boxes nor the teacher are coming back!"

The next day I went to the chorus room before school. Mrs. Hardaway was there, but thankfully the electrician was gone.

"Are you really leaving?" I asked.

She zipped over and closed the door.

"How did you hear that?" she asked.

I was embarrassed to tell her about the Fortune Wookiee, but she didn't really wait for an answer, anyway.

"Oh, Cassie, there are going to be so many changes, I just hate it. And I'm sorry I won't be here to help you through it all."

"What kind of changes?"

"Well," she said, "I guess I should let Ms. Rabbski explain that when the time comes. Basically, you guys are going to be busy with the fundamentals." And she said it like this: FUN-damentals.

"What does that mean?"

"Well, for starters it means no more chorus, and that means no more chorus teacher, and that means no more drama club, either . . . Don't tell anybody I told you this until after I'm gone, but . . . it . . . basically, it sucks."

And then she told me I was one of her favorites and that I would have made a great Olivia Twist. And I told

PLEASE, SIR... I WANT SOME MORE!

her that if we could figure out a way to do the play we would invite her to come back and see it. And she said she would love that. And she said some nice stuff about me and I said some nice stuff about her and then it was time for homeroom.

I'm glad Sara and her Fortune Wookiee solved the mystery, but I don't really like the solution very much. It seemed like with Origami Yoda everything kept turning out good, but this turned out bad. Who knows, maybe even Origami Yoda wouldn't be able to stop something like this?

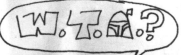

Harvey's Comment

What? Canceling chorus AND drama? What the Fett? But I'm signed up to take chorus next semester! And I was going to be awesome in that play, too.

And I have to admit, Sara is a pretty good detective.

My Comment: Harvey just said something nice about someone? Man, he must be shaken by the news about chorus and drama and all that.

The whole thing sounds kind of scary . . . .
FUN-damentals? Ugh.

Kellen's Comment

Uh, nobody panic, but I saw Mrs. Richards carrying
a bunch of boxes out of the art room!

ME

KELLEN'S CHAPTER

BY KELLEN

Tommy, I've got good news and bad news. The good news is I don't have to borrow my brother's recorder thingy anymore! He gave it to me when he got a phone that has a recording app and, uh, all this other stuff.

Recording thingy

So now I, uh, can tell my stories into the recorder anytime . . . and you just have to type them out. Uh, and edit out the "Uh"s. Thanks!

The bad news is that the Fortune Wookiee stinks! I mean, you know I totally believe in Origami Yoda, but the Fortune Wookiee is either just stupid or mean or worthless.

STINKS!   235   STUPID!   MEAN!

You know how Rhondella is still mad at me about that picture I drew—which I still say looked exactly like her or at least as close as I could get? Well, it's been driving me crazy. I've spent all these years trying to get Rhondella to like me, and I thought I was getting close, but now she's mad and so we're just stuck until I can figure out a way to make her unmad. Now this is exactly the sort of thing I would have asked Origami Yoda about. And I've been trying to ask Origami Yoda, but Dwight won't answer my e-mails.

Now everybody else was asking the Fortune Wookiee stuff and getting fairly good answers, but I didn't want to because of who you have to talk to to talk to the Fortune Wookiee: Sara, Rhondella's best friend. So I figured I'd have to figure out a way to make Rhondella unmad myself, but then I must have made a total mistake or something. I guess it was the Christmas present I gave her today. That part was Sara's advice, and I figured she was right: Instead of spending the money on myself, I'd spend it on Rhondella. I just had to decide what to get her. I remembered how much Sara liked that graphic novel you got her for her birthday, but I also remembered the big reaction Tater Tot got when he gave her that teddy bear.

So I got one of each for Rhondella. Since Rhondella loves Godzilla, I went down to Gypsy Witch Comics and got her this awesome *King of All Monsters* graphic novel, plus they had a stuffed animal Godzilla, which cost a lot because it was supposedly "vintage." But it was really, really cool! I carried them around in my backpack for three days, waiting for a chance to give them to her.

Then today in the library, you and Sara started whispering about something and Rhondella got annoyed and took her stuff and went over to the magazine shelf. *Finally,* I thought, *here's my chance.* But when I gave her the stuff, she acted like I was giving her chocolate-covered dog barf. I mean, you should have seen the look on her face. She said thanks, but with a fake smile, and she stuck them in her backpack without even looking at them and said she had to take them to her locker before class. And she just walked off! Well, I had psyched myself

CHOCOLATE COATING →

← DOUBLE DIPPED

up a lot just to give her the presents, so I still had enough left to go after her. She was walking real fast down the hall, and I was walking along right next to her, but she would hardly even look at me.

"Come on, Rhondella! Stop being mad at me. I'm sorry about the picture," I said.

She finally slowed down and looked at me. "I'm sorry, Kellen. I guess I'm being rude. Listen, I'm not mad at you anymore. Don't worry about it."

This would have made me really happy, but just the whole way she said it made me feel like things were even worse. And they were.

"Then what's the problem?" I asked.

"Maybe you should ask the Fortune Wookiee," she said. "Uh, I better go brush my hair. Thanks for the presents."

And she pushed her way through the kids going in the other direction and went across the hall and into the girls' bathroom.

I thought about waiting for her, but that seemed uncool, and I felt like I had already taken a bath in uncool.

Frankly, it didn't really seem so much better to give than to receive. In fact, it felt pretty spugly.

SPUGLY!

WHY?

So I went back to the library to talk to Sara. There was plenty of time left before homeroom; Rhondella had just used that as an excuse to get away. But why, man? If she wasn't mad about the picture anymore, then why? Sara was there talking to you—I'm sure you remember—and I asked her if I could talk to the Fortune Wookiee privately. And you were all, "Whine, whine, whine." And I was like, "Dude, this is important, so shut up for ten seconds." And you went off to play Pencil Wars with Lance.

So Sara said, "Do you have a decent question this time?"

"Yes, and I really need Chewie's help. Rhondella told me to ask."

"Okay, then," said Sara, and she got out Chewbacca and Han Foldo.

"All right," I started.

"Shhhh . . ." said Sara. "I think this needs to be a whisper conversation."

"Yeah, right," I whispered. "So Rhondella says she's not mad at me anymore, but she still treats me like an Ugnaught. The presents you told me to get her—"

"What? I never told you to get her a present!"

133

"But you said—"

"I meant, like, for your mom or somebody."

"Oh, well, I wish I had gotten something for my mom, because Rhondella barely even said thank you. She wasn't even nice. And when I asked her what the problem was, she said to ask the Fortune Wookiee."

Sara gave me a really nice smile and said, "Okay, let's see what he has to say . . ."

So we did the whole routine with the favorite movie and the counting and all and Sara moved Chewie's mouth open and closed for each number and she found the right flap and opened it up and Chewie made this pitiful kind of sound: "Wuuug."

"Wug?" I asked. "What's that mean?"

Sara held up Han Foldo. Han Foldo kind of shook his head back and forth. "I'm sorry, kid," said Han Foldo really softly. "Some things are just impossible."

"What's impossible?"

"I hate to tell you," Han said, "but Rhondella is impossible . . . for you."

"Wug!" said Chewie.

I looked at Sara.

"Really?"

"Wug," said Sara.

"But the Fortune Wookiee can tell me how to change that, right? How do I do it?"

"Shhh . . ." said Sara again. "You don't want everybody to hear this . . . The Fortune Wookiee has spoken. That's all he has to say."

"'Wug' is all he has to say? That stinks! Origami Yoda would figure out a way to change all this."

"No, Kellen," said Sara. "Origami Yoda would probably say, 'Search your feelings. True it is.'"

Then I said a word that was not "Bantha dung" but a different word that means basically the same thing, and I got up and left.

"Wait," said Sara. "Take this. Use it when you're feeling better."

She tried to give me a piece of origami.

"No thanks!" I shouted. I admit I was being really not nice. And I will apologize to Sara later. It's not her fault Dwight's stupid Fortune Wookiee doesn't work.

"Take it!" she ordered.

I took it. It was an origami Ewok. Great, just what I needed. I shoved it in my pocket.

The homeroom bell rang. It was the start of a very bad day.

A little bit ago, after I got home from school, I took a closer look at the origami Ewok. I wasn't really feeling better, but I was curious just in case there was some clue in there about how to get through to Rhondella. Maybe I was underestimating the power of Ewoks, just like everybody did in *Return of the Jedi*.

I pulled it out of my pocket and it had gotten kind of crumpled. I realized it was pretty awesome, and I wished I had taken better care of it. It was really well folded, and whoever made it had drawn a real good face on it. I realized it wasn't Dwight because Dwight just scrawls the face on his Yodas.

Then I looked on the back and there was a URL for photowallrus.com. So I typed it in. And this picture came up of me and this kind of cute girl standing in the library. It was the time I got that comic book award. I didn't realize it then, but the girl was giving me a huge smile in the picture. I wonder if she's the one who folded the Ewok?

But why did Sara give me this picture? What
does it have to do with Rhondella? And what
am I supposed to do about Rhondella?

I don't know, man, maybe the Fortune Wookiee
is right . . . WUG!

THINGS GET MUCH WEIRDER!!

BY TOMMY

Except for what happened to Kellen, the Fortune Wookiee seemed to be doing pretty good. Maybe not AS good as Origami Yoda, but pretty good.

I had tried to figure out how this was possible. I mean, Harvey is right when he points out that even the real Chewbacca didn't use the Force. So how can an origami Chewbacca use the Force? The best I could come up with was that maybe Dwight himself is the one who puts the Force into the origami.

ACTUAL JEDI!?

FORCE?

After all, I've folded several Yodas and none of them have talked. So maybe Dwight somehow puts the Force into his Yodas and somehow he figured out how to put the Force into Origami Chewbacca, too.

That was my best theory . . . until today when Harvey blew it completely out of the water.

Harvey did this total flip-out before school today . . . but the crazy thing is he may have been right. He wasn't right to flip out and embarrass all of us—again!—but he was maybe right about what he flipped out about.

It started with Harvey wanting to ask a question . . .

"Uh, Sara, I understand you had some secret advice for Kellen," Harvey said.

"Well, the Fortune Wookiee did," said Sara. She could tell right away that he was up to something, I think. He usually doesn't start conversations, he just butts into them. "But it was secret. I'm not going to tell you about it."

"No problem. I respect Kellen's privacy. I'd just like to see if Chewie and Han Foldo can help me, too. Can you do my fortune on the Fortune Wookiee?"

"Are you just going to make dumb comments about whatever it says?"

"I never make dumb comments," he said.

"Forget it," said Sara.

"No, that's not fair," said Harvey. "Dwight sent the Fortune Wookiee here to help all of us. Did he specifically say 'Don't let it help Harvey?'"

"No."

"Well, then it's not fair."

"Fine, what do you want advice about?"

"Anything."

"Anything?" asked Kellen. "Okay, Fortune Wookiee, tell Harvey how he can stop acting like a jerk all the time."

"Hey!"

"You said anything!"

"I don't act like a jerk all the time!"

"Yes, you do," said just about everybody
at the table, maybe everybody in the whole
library . . . maybe even the whole school!

I said it, too, but I was sorry right away
because I was afraid it was really going to
hurt his feelings. But Harvey seemed to be on
a mission. He plowed ahead.

"Okay, that gives me an idea for a better
question. Sara, ask the Fortune Wookiee why
everybody mistakenly thinks I'm a jerk,
please."

Sara got out the Fortune Wookiee. "Which
movie?"

"*The Empire Strikes Back*."

"One-two-three-four-five."

"Which character?"

"IG-88."

"Your favorite character is a robot that's
in the movie for, like, seven seconds and
doesn't do anything?"

"Yes. He has an awesome backstory that's not in the movie. See, he was manufactured on—"

"Okay! I-G-8-8."

Sara counted and lifted the fourth flap. She gave a sort of halfhearted "Mrrrrowwwwr."

"Mmm-hmmm," said Harvey. "And what does it say that means?"

"He says, 'Not everyone speaks Wookiee,'" said Han Foldo.

One second after that, all heck broke loose. But let me press the pause button so we can think about the Fortune Wookiee's answer . . . I've thought about it a lot since then, and I think that answer was actually really, really good.

I think Chewie was trying to tell Harvey that people don't always understand him. The words that come out of his mouth are kind of like Chewbacca's roars and stuff. They sound really harsh and awful.

But Chewbacca isn't harsh and awful, and

maybe Harvey isn't, either. His words are, but they don't mean the same thing to him that they mean to us. That's what Han meant by "Not everyone speaks Wookiee." Harvey needs to learn that not everyone understands him.

He criticizes and complains and hurts people's feelings all the time, but I think he would really be surprised if he knew that. He thinks he's just being funny or smart or even cool, but other people think he's acting like a jerk.

Unfortunately, Harvey didn't take any time to think about what Han Foldo meant, because he was too busy . . . acting like a jerk.

"AHA!" he shouted at Sara. "That's the ninth answer! The ninth DIFFERENT answer! The Fortune Wookiee has now given nine different answers to nine different people!"

"So what?" said Kellen.

"There are only eight flaps on a cootie catcher! Look . . ." And he tried to grab

the Fortune Wookiee from Sara. She held on tight and he held on tight and then Rhondella yanked on it and it ripped.

BLANK
FLAP

Harvey had half of it and he was pulling up the flaps and going, "Look, it doesn't say ANYTHING under these flaps! There are no fortunes here at all!"

Meanwhile, Rhondella was trying to grab his half back. Sara was just looking mad. Mrs. Calhoun came over and restored order. She made all of us boys move to a different table, except for Harvey, who had to go straight to his homeroom. She took both halves of the Fortune Wookiee and put them in her office.

"I hope Ms. Rabbski doesn't hear that I had to break up an origami-related fracas! She'll say origami should be banned from the library, too, and I won't be able to stop her this time."

We all agreed to cover it up and not talk about it.

But I was sure this wasn't over yet. I was

starting to think that Sara knew something
that we didn't.

Harvey's Comment

Well, I know what Sara knows. Why don't you
give me a chance to explain it all without being
interrupted?

My Comment: Be my guest . . .

Nuts

harvey

THE FORTUNE WOOKiEE THAT WASN'T

BY HARVEY

I was certain from the beginning that the Fortune Wookiee was a hoax, just like Origami Yoda. It was just Dwight trying to keep driving us crazy even though he's not here.

But this time I started to get some real evidence together. First: When Sara brought the Fortune Wookiee to school, she told us that Dwight had tossed him to her out his bedroom window. But later Tommy finds out that Dwight's windows are nailed shut.

Second: Did you notice that none of Sara's closest friends ever asked a question? Rhondella and Amy didn't bother asking, because they must have known it was a hoax, too.

Third: What are the chances that people would pick a different flap each time? It's against the odds. Sooner or later there should be a repeat. But there never was.

AND fourth: As I tried to say in the library, there are only eight flaps. But somehow there were nine answers. If I hadn't stopped her, there probably would have been even more.

That made it clear that Sara was just making stuff up. All that "What's your favorite movie," "Pick any character" stuff was just part of the act. Magicians call it misdirection.

So there's your PRoof! Not my opinion this time, but actual PRoof!

So put that in your case file, Tommy!

My Comment: I am putting it in the case file, dude. Just relax!

To tell you the truth, I think you're right this time.

I believe you. I don't want to, but I do. I've gone back over every story in this case file now, and it really seems like this whole thing has been a trick.

But the thing I'm not sure about is whether this was just Dwight or whether Sara has been lying to us this whole time, too. I mean, if Dwight fooled Sara, that's one thing. But if Sara's friends knew it was a hoax, then Sara must have known it was a hoax. And if she was making up the answers, then she DEFINITELY knew it was a hoax.

So what the heck has been going on around here?

There's only one way to finish this case file. I've got to confront Sara with Harvey's evidence and find out.

Here I go . . .

SARA BOLT... WOMAN OF MYSTERY!?

Me: So, Sara, do you mind if we use Kellen's recorder thingy for this? You know, for the case file?

Sara: You can use it, but I don't think you're going to want to put this in the case file.

Me: But I thought you said you would explain it all.

Sara: Oh, I'll explain it all, but you're not going to like it, and you're not going to want to let Kellen see it, either.

Me: Kellen? Why not?

Sara: You'll see. Just start asking ques-
        tions.

Me: Okay. So what is the deal with the
        Fortune Wookiee? It seems like this
        time Dwight was just tricking us.

Sara: Actually, Dwight wasn't tricking you
        at all. Dwight doesn't have anything
        to do with this. He didn't even make
        it. I did.

Me: YOU MADE IT?

Sara: Yeah, Han Foldo, too.

Me: The whole thing was your idea?

Sara: Actually, it was all Rhondella's
        idea at first. This is the part Kellen
        doesn't need to know about. See, the
        whole reason for the Fortune Wookiee
        was just to give Kellen that answer.

Me: The whole thing was just to break
        Kellen's heart?

Sara: No! The opposite. See, right after
        Dwight left, Rhondella said something

like, "You know, I was finally starting to believe in Origami Yoda. I was going to ask him how I could get rid of Kellen—you know, without hurting his feelings. You know, something like, 'Like you that way she does not. Friends just be she wants. Over it you must get.' He would have listened to Yoda." So, then her and me and Amy cooked up the idea for the Fortune Wookiee.

Me: Why Chewie? If it was a girl thing, why didn't you make Origami Princess Leia?

Sara: Would you have listened to Princess Leia? I wasn't sure, but I knew you'd listen to Chewbacca . . . Plus, I do an awesome Chewbacca imitation. MMMWWWWRGGGGHHHHHHH!

Me: Yeah, it is pretty amazing.

Sara: The only problem we had was that Kellen kept asking the wrong questions. But

I figured he would finally get around to asking about Rhondella, and he did. And in the meantime, I found out that Remi liked him, so we were able to throw that in as a little ray of hope for the poor dude. But we also had to make it clear—he was never going to get Rhondella.

Me: NOOOOOO! That's totally not fair! Origami Yoda would have HELPED Kellen, and you were supposed to help him, too.

Sara: I did help him. He needed to know that Rhondella and him just isn't going to happen. But Remi . . . That can happen if he just stops pestering Rhondella long enough to look around.

Me: But Kellen has been in love with Rhondella since third grade! He's not just going to change to Remi in two seconds.

Sara: That's the whole problem. Kellen isn't in love with the real Rhondella, he's in love with the Rhondella he knew in third grade, back when she liked Godzilla.

Me: You mean she doesn't like Godzilla anymore? She used to talk about monster movies all the time.

Sara: Yeah, USED TO. When's the last time you heard her say anything about Godzilla? She's totally changed since then. Unlike Kellen, she's been growing up. And Kellen hasn't been paying attention because he decided he loved her in third grade and hasn't even thought about it since then. But the seventh grade Rhondella doesn't like Godzilla . . . or Kellen. And she never will.

Me: Ouch.

Sara: But Remi does! Well, she likes manga

more than monster movies, but close enough, and she does like Kellen. A lot. And I think that's all he needed to know to get unstuck from Rhondella.

Me: Wow. Okay, even if I accept for a minute that your answer to Kellen was a good one . . . what about the other answers? Like the meat loaf and you acting like Sherlock Holmes and me having to apologize to Harvey.

Sara: Everything else was just misdirection, as Harvey called it. Kind of ticks me off that he's right. But he was right.

Me: You're ticked off? I'M ticked off! You made me apologize to Harvey! We trusted you!

Sara: Well, it WAS good advice. You did need to apologize. It was all good advice, especially that meat loaf one. I'm pretty proud of that. It

	just popped into my head. You see, the Force isn't the only force around here.
Me:	What else?
Sara:	Girl Power!
Me:	So basically all of us boys have just been doing what you girls wanted us to do for the last month?
Sara:	Yes. Worked out pretty good, didn't it? In fact, I'd say we're totally Jedi wise!

My Comment: Well, I won't be putting this in the case file, that's for sure. This will go in the SECRET case file, along with Remi's chapter. Kellen doesn't need to know, and Harvey sure doesn't need to know, either. But I think it's only right that I add something to the case file to explain what the truth really was . . .

THE SECRET OF THE FORTUNE WOOKIEE

BY TOMMY

The Fortune Wookiee was not using the Force, not making real predictions, and not actually made by Dwight. Sara made it herself and made up the predictions, too.

I WAS RIGHT

BY HARVEY

I was right! I was right! I was right! I was right!
I was right! I was right! I was right! I was right!
I was right! I was right! I was right! I was right!
I was right! I was right! I was right! I was right!
I was right! I was right! I was right! I was right!
I was right! I was right! I was right! I was right!
I was right! I was right! I was right! I was right!
I was right! I was right! I was right! I was right!
I was right! I was right! I was right! I was right!
I was right! I was right! I was right! I was right!
I was right! I was right! I was right! I was right!

I was right! I was right! I was right! I was right! I was right! I was right!

Harvey's Comment

But I do have to admit I was surprised that this was all Sara and no Dwight. I think I underestimated her!

My Comment: Me, too!

SO....
I GUESS
THIS MEANS...

YEAH...
SORRY,
KID.

DWIGHT AT TIPPETT ACADEMY

BY CAROLINE

Okay, Tommy, here is my chapter about Dwight at Tippett Academy. If this doesn't convince you to do something, then I don't know what to do. You're my only hope! And that's not just a movie line.

Remember one time you wrote in your case file that "Dwight is whatever it is he is"?

Well, he's NOT anymore. He's Not Dwight.

Not Dwight is zero percent fun and zero percent weird and zero percent Dwight!

I think this school is destroying the real Dwight! And if it's this bad after just a month and a half, how bad is it going to be after the whole school year?

NOT DWIGHT — 100%!!

DWIGHT 0%

It's hard to write a chapter about what he's doing that's wrong, because he really doesn't do much. It's more the things he doesn't do.

He doesn't cause problems in assemblies like he used to. He just sits there. (By the way, did you know that Mr. Good Clean Fun comes to Tippett, too? There's no escape!)

He doesn't lie down in strange places—like second base on the kickball field. He just sits or stands quietly and does what he's told.

He doesn't fold origami in class—or anywhere else, as far as I can tell.

He doesn't do anything that might get him into any trouble. I think he's terrified of getting in trouble and getting his mom all worked up again. So he's decided not to do anything of interest at all.

And one of the things that bothers me the most is that he doesn't avoid the obnoxious kids. I've told you before about how Tippett is all about Understanding Our Differences and how some of the kids are really, really annoying because they insist on Understanding you all the time.

The old Dwight wouldn't have put up with that. But Not Dwight almost seems to like it. I think he thinks he's fitting in, but these kids don't really understand him, they just Understand him.

KIMMY   HEATHER

I know that doesn't make much sense, so I actually talked to a couple of these girls to try to help you understand.

It wasn't pleasant! These girls are huggers! If they would just hug each other that would be fine, but they are always trying to hug other people. One of them even tried to hug me once. And they are always trying to hug Dwight.

Well, you may not know this, but Dwight HATES to be hugged. He doesn't even like me to hug him—so I don't!

But nothing can stop these two girls who are named Kimmy and Heather.

Me: "Guys, I saw you earlier hugging Dwight . . ."

Kimmy: "Isn't he sweet? We just love Dwight!"

Me: "But you shouldn't hug him."

Heather: "Why not? Everyone needs a hug sometimes."

Me: "No, not everyone. Listen, Dwight is different."

Heather: "Yeah, we know! He's special, and that's why he needs an extra hug sometimes."

Me: "Don't call him special. He's not special!"

Heather and Kimmy: <<GASP!>>

Kimmy: "I thought you were supposed to be Dwight's friend!"

Me: "I am!"

Kimmy: "But I don't think you're being very nice to Dwight! And it's important to be nice to Dwight. He's special."

Me: "If you call him 'special' one more time, I'm going to clobber you!"

Heather: "I think you have a problem Understanding Our Differences!"

Kimmy: "Yeah, me, too!"

And they stomped off, probably to go hug Dwight some more!

Well, does that clear things up? Are you starting to see what things are like for Dwight here at Tippett?

Everybody claims to "just love" him, but he doesn't have any real friends as far as I can tell.

Tommy, I know that you are his real friend. That's why I'm hoping this case file helps you figure out a way to help him. I've tried to talk to him about it, but he just keeps saying that everything is okay.

Nobody treats him like a real person. More like a class pet. And frankly, I think he's so afraid to get in trouble again that he's acting like one. Even worse, I think he's starting to like it. It must be kind of nice to have everyone pat you on the head and vote for your crappy library poster (you saw the poster, right?) and say everything you do is "just great" and call you "special" all the time.

And as for Origami Yoda ... forget it! They all have their

GOOD DWIGHT!

SOMEONE SAVE ME!

LOOK! PAPER CLIP EARRINGS YOU MUST WEAR!

own Yodas and do the DUMBEST possible stuff with them. No one here REALLY believes in Origami Yoda ... except me. I'm not even sure Dwight believes anymore.

Tommy, the real Dwight is disappearing! And Not Dwight is zero fun.

Pretty soon he won't be weird and he won't even be special ... he'll just be boring. And I think he'll be miserable. I know I will be.

What do you think, Tommy? Do you think you can help him?

Harvey's Comment

I know I used to wish Dwight would not be so weird ... but I never meant for him to turn all normal on us.

And I can't believe he's letting those huggy girls anywhere near him! They are scary-Scoob-scary!

My Comment: Well, I think they probably mean well, but you're right: They are scary!

And now I can see how wrong I was about Dwight being "fixed." If he's acting this normal, then that means he's broken.

We've got to help him . . . but I have no idea how.

SOMEONE SAVE ME!

HAN FOLDO'S ADVICE

BY TOMMY

So I was telling Sara about all this and about how I had no idea how to help Dwight.

"I wish I could ask Origami Yoda," I said. "Or the Fortune Wookiee, if it wasn't a fake—and ripped up."

"Well," she said, "you could always ask Han Foldo . . ."

"But he's fake, too."

"Who you calling fake, kid?" asked Han Foldo, who Sara had just put on her finger.

"Uh, Sara, I'm serious."

"So is Han Foldo," said Sara.

Sometimes I wonder if all of my friends are insane.

"All right, what does Han Foldo think?"

"It's obvious, kid," said Han. "Dwight has to get out of that dump and move back here to McQuarrie."

"That would be great," I said. "But he doesn't want to come back. He claims to like Tippett better!"

"Well, then I guess you're just going to have to go get him."

JUMP TO LIGHTSPEED, CHEWIE!

ORIGAMI YODA AND DWIGHT

BY TOMMY

I went back to see Dwight.

He gave me the same hassle about getting in, and I had to crawl through the doggie door again. Maybe that's why I may have sounded a bit harsh. Plus I was trying to do this Han Solo-style.

"I think it's an act, Dwight," I said, pushing past him and going up the stairs to his room.

"What?"

"All this Bantha dung about you winning

ENOUGH w7TH THE BANTHA DUM JOKES!!

poster contests and getting hugged all the time and being a good little boy. It's an act."

"Well, I *am* trying to act better."

"Yeah, I've heard. The problem is you're acting like a weenie."

weenie
DWIGHT.

"But everybody likes me now," he said.

He followed me into his room. I turned on him and let him have it.

"Caroline doesn't. And I don't. And Origami Yoda doesn't."

"What?"

"Do you even remember Origami Yoda? And I'm not talking about those clones your new 'friends' made, I'm talking about the real Origami Yoda. Get him out of the frame. Let's ask him."

"I told you, he's hard to get out," he mumbled.

"Fine, I'll do it," I said. I took the picture frame off the wall. I almost ripped out a fingernail trying to pry open the back of the frame. But I got it loose, and the

167

glass and some fancy cardboard and Origami Yoda all popped out.

I tried to hand Origami Yoda to Dwight. He wouldn't take him. I saw that I had scared him a little. He was starting to shut down on me. I told myself to relax.

"You want to hear what Origami Yoda says, Dwight?"

"Okay," he said, and I knew I wasn't too late.

I put Origami Yoda on my own finger.

"Luminous beings are we, not this crude matter."

"What does he mean?" asked Dwight, and he actually seemed interested.

"I'm not sure," I said. "I didn't really mean to say that."

And I don't think I really did. It just popped out. It is one of the weirdest Yoda lines from any of the movies. It made no sense to me at all until I found out that "luminous" means "glowing." And then it was still confusing. Until now.

"I think Origami Yoda is saying that you're supposed to be luminous . . . to be awesome, not boring.

"You're supposed to have Origami Yoda and eat Rib-B-Qs and sit in holes. You're supposed to fight with Harvey and drive me crazy by saying 'purple' over and over. Maybe you're even supposed to get into trouble with Ms. Rabbski."

PURPLE!

I looked over at Dwight and saw that he was looking right at me. He almost never looks right at you.

"What you're not supposed to be is a class pet for those Tippett kids, and that's what Caroline says you are. They're too busy calling you 'special' to realize that you're awesome. Aren't you sick of that?"

"Well, sort of. But it's better than—"

"No, it's not," I said. "Anyway, you need to read this before you say anything else."

"What is it?"

"It's a mini-case file. We made it for you."

THE DWIGHT FILE

Dwight sat there for a long time. Just sort of staring at the plastic anchor. I decided to give him time to think. So I just sat there, looking at Origami Yoda up close. Thinking about what a genius Dwight was to have made it in the first place, and remembering how it had changed everything at McQuarrie. And how the kids at Tippett had totally missed out on all that.

Origami Yoda had saved us, and now I hoped he would save Dwight.

I held up Origami Yoda and tried to make him say the perfect thing one more time:

"Easy it is at Tippett," said Origami Yoda/me. "But easy life is supposed not to be." I realized that didn't sound very Yoda-like.

"Or not supposed to be easy life is not . . . Or . . . Uh . . ."

A minute ago I had just somehow known what Origami Yoda should say; now I couldn't seem to get it to work.

"Can I have him?" Dwight asked.

I handed over Origami Yoda. Dwight put him on his finger. They looked at each other for a minute. Then Dwight nodded.

"Boring being normal is," said Origami Yoda.

"Yeah," said Dwight, "and being 'special' just stinks."

"So why don't you just come back and be Dwight again?" I asked.

"Purple," said Dwight. And he was actually smiling for once, so I knew he meant yes.

I jumped up to give him a high five or hug him or something, then I remembered what Caroline had said.

So I just said, "Stooky!"

But then Dwight stopped smiling and lifted up Origami Yoda. He started doing that other Yoda voice. Not the really lame Yoda impression, but the voice that sounds like Yoda when Yoda is totally scary-serious and sensing the Dark Side.

"Yes . . . at McQuarrie we belong. Return

we must. Need us you will . . . all of you. A great battle ahead I sense."

"A battle with who?"

"Rabbski!"

"Oh, just relax about Rabbski. I'm not scared of her."

Origami Yoda shook his tiny paper head.

"You will be . . . You will be . . ."

HAPPY NEW YEAR FROM RABBSKI

BY TOMMY

Well, that conversation with Dwight was weird and confusing, but not boring . . . so I guess things are back to normal at last.

After I was done at Dwight's, I stopped next door to see if Sara was home. She was. We sat at her kitchen counter eating a giant bowlful of Chex Mix her mom had made and talked about a bunch of stuff, but of course the first thing I told her was about Dwight coming back.

"That's awesome," she said.

"Yeah, but I'm worried that he's going to

get in trouble again. Origami Yoda said there was going to be a battle with Rabbski. The weird thing is he made it sound like we would all be in it."

"Uh-oh," said Sara. "That reminds me of the letter we got this morning. Did you get it yet?"

"What letter?"

There was a pile of mail in a box at the end of the counter under the phone. She pulled out a letter to parents from Mrs. Rabbski about changes at McQuarrie next semester.

"What?!?!?" I gasped. "Replacing electives with 'Preparation and Review periods'? That's supposed to be FUN?"

"See," said Sara, "this explains what was going on with the chorus teacher AND the art teacher! We're going to be too busy reviewing for those dumb tests to put on a play or paint or build LEGO robots or anything. Can you imagine how boring those reviews are going to be?"

Dear Parent,

There are going to be a lot of changes taking place at McQuarrie when the new semester begins January 11.

I know many of you have been concerned about the unsatisfactory performance of McQuarrie students on our state Standards of Learning test. Be assured that school administrators have been working hard to fix this problem. Now it is time for your child(ren) to work hard with us.

On January 11, we will launch our new core curriculum, "FUNTIME™! Time to Focus on the FUN-damentals!" FUNTIME™ is a very successful educational program developed by Edu-Fun Products, a leader in the field of test score improvement.

As the title suggests, McQuarrie will be focusing on improving student test scores in fundamental testing areas, such as math and reading comprehension. Elective courses, such as art, chorus, band, domestic science, etc., will be replaced by FUNTIME™ Test Preparation and Review periods.

While your child(ren) may be disappointed at first, we believe that all students will soon find that, with this new educational program, they'll have a FUN TIME finding the FUN in FUN-damentals! And together we will put McQuarrie where it belongs: at the TOP of the Standards of Learning testing list!

If you have any questions, feel free to contact my office.

Lougene Rabbski
Principal
McQuarrie Middle School

"Origami Yoda was right!" I said. "I AM scared! This is going to be a whole new level of boring."

"The Fortune Wookiee has something to say about it, too," said Sara.

Chewie and Han Foldo were stuck to her refrigerator with magnets. She pulled off Chewie—who she had taped back together—and made him talk:

"WUG!"

I pulled off Han Foldo and made him say the only thing left to say:

"I have a bad feeling about this."

THE END

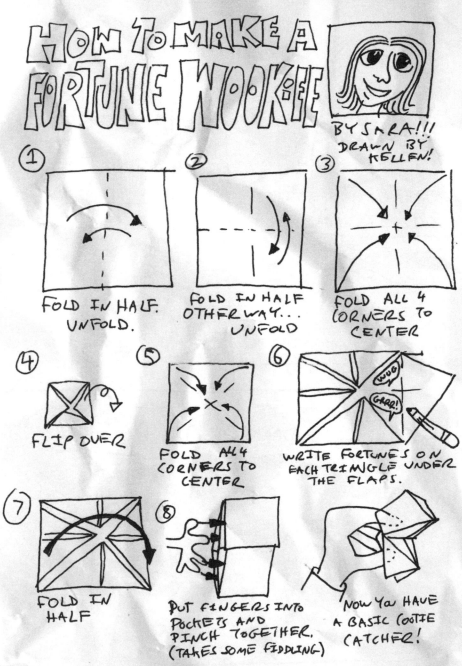

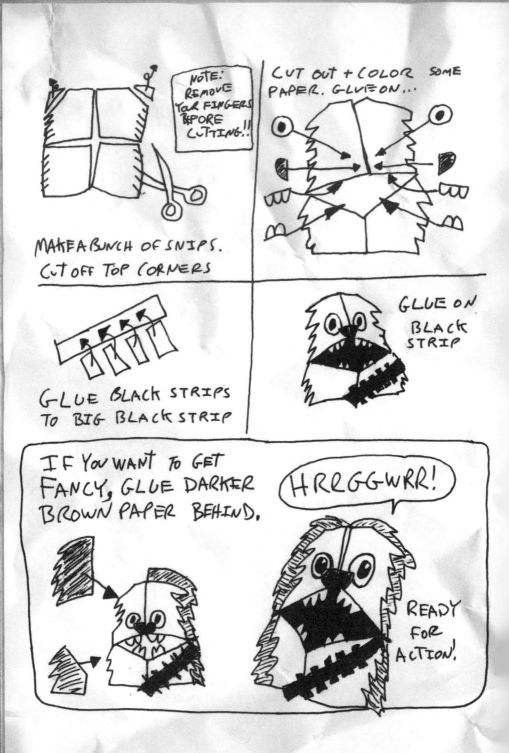

ACKNOWLEDGMENTS

The SuperFolders: Oscar, Charlie, Michael, Elayna, Mia, AustinM, ChadY, ChadH, Zach, Kate, Gavin, Mikey, Peyton, WyattL, Darby, DT, Teddy, WyattP, Samuel, Sean, Yonatan, JC, Megan/Phred, Fer, Rocket, Tayler, Graham, Karina, OrigamiYodaHelper, Sam, Seb, Michelle, Stevie, Juan, DJ, Yodamaster, BobaFett1212, Yoda, Henry, JackB, JackT, SamM, Artoo, Ethan, ClaytonH, Andrew, Jake, Rymit, Daniel, Hubert, GavinW, Ashton, Kody, Quinn, OscarH, OscarU, Simon, Wicket, JackL, Caden, Houston, Haviland, EvanS, Troy, Samigami1221, Wes, JackB, Damien, Filip, HenryF, Evil Jawa, Lonefish Josh, Joey, Saul, EthanB, Siavash,

The Three Yodateers, Fettman, Tenor, Javier, ToxicTony, Alex, Varun, CharlieB, SMSGuysRead, TMCGuysRead, Gingka, Aaron, Hansen, John F, Kevin, Kaleb, DBZFan, Bobby, UmHiGuy, Brandon, Joseph, Holly, Yann, Nico, Marcus, Cam, Jamin, MichaelT, Nicholas, Rishi, Tyler 138, Daniel, Justin, Robby, Simon, Angus, Lord of the Folds, The Origami Yoda Investigators, The Yellow Roomers, The StarWarigami Club, JG, JSWP, Evan, TeddyR, Jeffrey, Treveleyan, Joshua, Jean-Paul, TeddyL, SamM, Nathan, Eash, AfroOrigamiMan, Scott, Jarod, Zach, Zeb, Harrison, JoeJoe, Mark, Edward, Dennis, Colin, Frank, Crispin, Sesuj, all the Larrys, Xarl, Noah, all the SuperFolders listed in Darth Paper, and everyone else who has sent in their origami and art to origamiyoda.com!

The SuperFolder Council: Samy, Ben, Chris Alexander, Fumiaki Kawahata, and Van Jahnke.

SuperDrawers: Jason Rosenstock, Cece Bell, Bonnie Burton, and Diego.

SuperAuthors: Eric Wight, Kirby Larson,

Jenni Holm, John Claude Bemis, Michael Buckley, Lisa Yee, Jack Ferraiolo, Grace Lin, Jonathan Auxier, Adam Rex, Dan Santat, Amy Ignatow, Adam Gidwitz, Jon Scieszka, and Jeff Kinney.

Super Booksellers, Librarians, Teachers, Reading Specialists, and Principals, including: Carla, Judy, Linda, T.J., Olga, Patti, Colby, Mr. Schu, Donalyn, TheNerdyBookClub, Anita, Cindy, Paula & Co., MichelleW, T.R. Kravtin, and Brian Compton aka Mr. GoodCleanFun.

SuperFriends and SuperRelations: Will, Rhonda, The Great Wastoli, the Hemphills, Webmaster Sam, Barbara and George, Grace, Ethel, and my parents, Wayne and Mary Ann Angleberger.

The SuperSquadron at Abrams/Amulet: Susan, Chad, Melissa, Jason, Laura, Erica, Jim, Elisa, Mary, and Michael.

TheSuperFolks at Scholastic and Scholastic Bookfairs and Recorded Books, especially the audiobook voice of Tommy, Mark Turetsky.

SuperInspiringStuff: Episodes I thru VI, The Clone Wars, Gregory's Girl, The Band, Godzilla, Dr. Who, Daniel Pinkwater, the State of Texas, and LEGOs.

The SuperMovieMakers at Lucasfilm: George Lucas, Peter Mayhew, Harrison Ford, Frank Oz, Warwick Davis, Ralph McQuarrie, Lawrence Kasdan, Kristen and Pablo Hidalgo, J.W. Rinzler, and Carol Roeder.

And my constant collaborator, Superstar Cece Bell.

ABOUT THE AUTHOR

Tom Angleberger is the author of the *New York Times* bestselling Origami Yoda series, which includes *The Strange Case of Origami Yoda* and *Darth Paper Strikes Back*. He is also the author of *Fake Mustache* and *Horton Halfpott*, an Edgar Award nominee. Visit him online at www.origamiyoda.com. Tom lives in the Appalachian Mountains of Virginia.

This book was designed by Melissa J. Arnst and art directed by Chad W. Beckerman. The main text is set in 10-point Lucida Sans Typewriter. The display typeface is ERASER. Tommy's comments are set in Kienan, and Harvey's comments are set in Good Dog. The hand lettering on the cover was done by Jason Rosenstock.

This book was printed and bound by R.R. Donnelley in Crawfordsville, Indiana. Its production was overseen by Alison Gervais